HALLDÓR LAXNESS

UNDER THE GLACIER

Halldór Laxness was born near Reykjavík, Iceland, in 1902. His first novel was published when he was seventeen. The undisputed master of contemporary Icelandic fiction, and one of the outstanding novelists of the century, he wrote more than sixty books, including novels, short stories, essays, poems, plays, and memoirs. In 1955 he was awarded the Nobel Prize in Literature. Laxness died in 1998.

INTERNATIONAL

UNDER THE GLACIER

HALLDÓR LAXNESS

*Translated from the Icelandic
by Magnus Magnusson*

Introduction by Susan Sontag

VINTAGE INTERNATIONAL

VINTAGE BOOKS

A DIVISION OF RANDOM HOUSE, INC.

NEW YORK

A VINTAGE INTERNATIONAL ORIGINAL, FEBRUARY 2005

Library of Congress Cataloging-in-Publication Data
Halldór Laxness, 1902–1998
[Kristnihald undir jökli. English]
Under the glacier / Halldór Laxness ; translated from the Icelandic by
Magnus Magnusson; introduction by Susan Sontag.
p. cm.
ISBN 1-4000-3441-8 (trade pbk.)
I. Magnusson, Magnus. II. Title.
PT7511.L3K713   2004
839'.6935—dc22   2004043086

Book design by Mia Risberg

www.vintagebooks.com

Printed in the United States of America
10 9 8 7 6 5 4 3

Outlandish

The long prose fiction called the novel, for want of a better name, has yet to shake off the mandate of its own normality as promulgated in the nineteenth century: to tell a story peopled by characters whose options and destinies are those of ordinary, so-called real life. Narratives that deviate from this artificial norm and tell other kinds of stories, or appear not to tell much of a story at all, draw on traditions that are more venerable than those of the nineteenth century, but still, to this day, seem innovative or ultra-literary or bizarre. I am thinking of novels that proceed largely through dialogue; novels that are relentlessly jocular (and therefore seem exaggerated) or didactic; novels whose characters spend most of their time musing to themselves or debating with a captive interlocutor about spiritual and intellectual issues; novels that tell of the initiation of an ingenuous young person into mystifying wisdom or revelatory abjection; novels with characters who have supernatural options, like shape-shifting and resurrection; novels that evoke imaginary geography. It seems odd to describe *Gulliver's Travels* or *Candide* or *Tristram Shandy* or *Jacques the Fatalist and His Master* or *Alice in Wonderland* or Gershenzon and Ivanov's *Correspondence from Two Corners* or Kafka's *The Castle* or Hesse's

Steppenwolf or Woolf's *The Waves* or Olaf Stapledon's *Odd John* or Gombrowicz's *Ferdydurke* or Calvino's *Invisible Cities* or, for that matter, porno narratives simply as novels. To make the point that these occupy the outlying precincts of the novel's main tradition, special labels are invoked.

Science fiction.

Tale, fable, allegory.

Philosophical novel.

Dream novel.

Visionary novel.

Literature of fantasy.

Wisdom lit.

Spoof.

Sexual turn-on.

Convention dictates that we slot many of the last centuries' perdurable literary achievements into one or another of these categories.

The only novel I know that fits into all of them is Halldór Laxness's wildly original, morose, uproarious *Under the Glacier*.

Science fiction first.

In 1864 Jules Verne published *Journey to the Center of the Earth*, the charming narrative of the adventures of a party of three, led by a German professor of mineralogy—the irascible mad-scientist type—who have lowered themselves into an extinct volcanic crater on a glacier in Iceland, Snæfells, and eventually exit upward through the mouth of an active volcano on another island, Stromboli, off the coast of Sicily. Just over a hundred years later, in 1968, Snæfells is again the designated portal of another unlikely fictional mission in a novel by Iceland's own Halldór Laxness, written with full mocking awareness of how the French father of science fiction had colonized the Icelandic site. This time, instead of a journey into the earth, mere proximity to the glacier opens up access to unexpected, cosmic mysteries.

Imagining the exceptional, often understood as the miraculous, the magical, or the supernatural, is a perennial job of storytelling. One tradition proposes a physical place of entry—a cave or a tunnel or a hole—which leads to a freakish or enchanted kingdom with an alternative normality. In Laxness's story, a sojourn near Snæfells does not call for the derring-do of a descent, a penetration, since, as Icelanders who inhabit the region know, the glacier itself is the center of the universe. The supernatural—the center—is present on the surface, in the costume of everyday life in a village whose errant pastor has ceased to conduct services or baptize children or bury the dead. Christianity—Iceland's confession is Evangelical Lutheran—is the name of what is normal, historical, local.* (The agricultural Viking island converted to Christianity on a single day at the Althing, the world's oldest national parliament, in 999.) But what is happening in remote Snæfells is abnormal, cosmic, global.

Science fiction proposes two essential challenges to conventional ideas of time and place. One is that time may be abridged, or become "unreal." The other is that there are special places in the universe where familiar laws that govern identity and morality are violated. In more strenuous forms of science fiction, these are places where good and evil contend. In benign versions of this geographical exceptionalism, these are places where wisdom accumulates. Snæfells is such a place—or so it is stipulated. People lead their mundane, peculiar lives, seemingly unfazed by the knowledge of the uniqueness of where they live: "No one in these parts doubts that the glacier is the centre of the universe." Snæfells has become a laboratory of the new, the unsettling: a place of secret pilgrimage.

---

* A literal translation of the original Icelandic title is *Christianity at Glacier*.

. . .

As a species of storytelling, science fiction is a modern variant of the literature of allegorical quest. It often takes the form of a perilous or mysterious journey, recounted by a venturesome but ignorant traveler who braves the obstacles to confront another reality that is charged with revelations. He—for it is always a he—stands for humanity as apprenticeship, since women are not thought to be representative of human beings in general but only of women. A woman can represent Women. Only a man can stand for Man or Mankind—everybody. Of course, a female protagonist can represent The Child—as in *Alice in Wonderland*—but not The Adult.

Thus, both *Journey to the Center of the Earth* and *Under the Glacier* have as their protagonists and narrators a good-natured, naive young man who submits his will to that of an older authority figure. Verne's narrator is the eminent Professor Lidenbrock's orphaned nephew and assistant, Axel, who cannot refuse the invitation to accompany his uncle and an Icelandic guide on this adventure, though he is sure that it will cost them their lives. In Laxness's novel, which opens on a note of parody, the narrator is a nameless youth whom the bishop of Iceland in Reykjavík wants to send to the village at the foot of Snæfells Glacier "to conduct the most important investigation at that world-famous mountain since the days of Jules Verne." He is to find out what has happened to the parish there, whose minister—pastor Jón Jónsson, known as Prímus—has not drawn his salary for twenty years. Is Christianity still being practiced? There are rumors that the church is boarded up and no services held, that the pastor lives with someone who is not his wife, that he has allowed a corpse to be lodged in the glacier.

The bishop tells the young man he has sent countless letters to Prímus. No answer. He wants the young man to make a brief trip to the village, talk to the pastor, and take the true measure of his spiritual dereliction.

And beyond science fiction:

Under the Glacier is at least as much a philosophical novel and a dream novel. It is also one of the funniest books ever written. But these genres—science fiction, philosophical novel, dream novel, comic novel—are not as distinct as one might suppose.

For instance, both science fictions and philosophical novels need principal characters who are skeptical, recalcitrant, astonished, ready to marvel. The science fiction novel usually begins with the proposal of a journey. The philosophical novel may dispense with the journey—thinking is a sedentary occupation—but not with the classical male pair: the master who asks and the servant who is certain, the one who is puzzled and the one who thinks he has the answers.

In the science fiction novel, the protagonist must first contend with his terrors. Axel's dread at being enrolled by his uncle in this daft venture of descending into the bowels of the earth is more than understandable. The question is not what he will learn but whether he will survive the physical shocks to which he will be subjected. In the philosophical novel, the element of fear—and true danger—is minimal, if it exists at all. The question is not survival but what one can know, and if one can know anything at all. Indeed, the very conditions of knowing become the subject of rumination.

In *Under the Glacier*, when the generic Naive Young Man receives his charge from the bishop of Iceland to investigate the goings-on at Snæfells, he protests that he is completely unqualified for the mission. In particular—"for the sake of appearances," he adds slyly—he instances his youth and lack of authority to scrutinize a venerable old man's discharge of his pastoral duties, when the words of the bishop himself have been ignored. Is the young man—the reader is told that he is twenty-five and a student—at least a theological student? Not even. Has he plans to be ordained? Not really. Is he married? No. (In fact, as we learn, he's a virgin.) A problem then? No problem. To the worldly bishop, the lack of qualifications of this Candide-like young Icelander is what makes him the right person. If the young man were qualified, he might be tempted to judge what he sees.

All the young man has to do, the bishop explains, is keep his eyes open, listen, and take notes; that the bishop knows he can do, having observed the young man take notes in shorthand at a recent synod meeting, and also using the—what's it called? a phonograph? It was a tape recorder, says the young man. And then, the bishop continues, write it all up. What you saw and heard. Don't judge.

Laxness's novel is both the narrative of the journey and the report.

A philosophical novel generally proceeds by setting up a quarrel with the very notion of novelistic invention. One common device is to present the fiction as a document, something found or recovered, often after its author's death or disappearance: research or writings in manuscript, a diary, a cache of letters.

In *Under the Glacier*, the anti-fictional fiction is that what the reader has in hand is a document prepared or in preparation, submitted rather than found. Laxness's ingenious design deploys two notions of "a report": the report to the reader, sometimes in the first person, sometimes in the form of unadorned dialogue, which is cast as the material, culled from taped conversations and observations from shorthand notebooks, of a report that is yet to be written up and presented to the bishop. The status of Laxness's narrative is something like a Moebius strip: report to the reader and report to the bishop continue to inflect each other. The first-person voice is actually a hybrid voice; the young man—whose name is never divulged—frequently refers to himself in the third person. "The undersigned" he calls himself at first. Then "Emissary of the Bishop," abbreviated to "EmBi," which quickly becomes "Embi." And he remains the undersigned or Embi throughout the novel.

The arrival of the emissary of the bishop of Iceland is expected, Embi learns when he reaches the remote village by bus one spring day; it's early May. From the beginning, Embi's picturesque informants, secretive and garrulous in the usual rural ways, accept his right to interrogate them without either curiosity or antagonism. Indeed, one running gag in the novel is that the villagers tend to address him as "bishop." When he protests that he is a mere emissary, they reply that his role makes him spiritually consubstantial with the bishop. Bishop's emissary, bishop—same thing.

And so this earnest, self-effacing young man—who refers to himself in the third person, out of modesty, not for the usual reason—moves from conversation to conversation, for this is a novel of talk, debate, sparring, rumination. Everyone whom he interviews has pagan or post-Christian ideas about time and obligation and the energies of the universe: the little village at the foot of a glacier is in full spiritual molt. Present, in addition to elusive pastor Jón—who, when Embi finally catches up with him (he now earns a living as the jack-of-all-trades for the whole district), shocks the youth with his sly theological observations—is an international conclave of gurus, the most eminent of which is Dr. Godman Syngmann from Ojai, California. Embi does not aspire to be initiated into any of these heresies. He wishes to remain a guest, an observer, an amanuensis: his task is to be a mirror. But when eros enters in the form of the pastor's mysterious wife, Úa, he becomes—first reluctantly, then surrendering eagerly—a participant. He wants something. Longing erupts. It becomes his journey, his initiation, after all. ("The report has not just become part of my own blood—the quick of my life has fused into one with the report.") The journey ends when the revelatory presence proves to be a phantom, and vanishes. The utopia of erotic transformation was only a dream, after all. But it is hard to undo an initiation. The protagonist will have to labor to return to reality.

Dream novel.

Readers will recognize the distinctive dream world of Scandinavian folk mythology, in which the spiritual quest of a male is empowered and sustained by the generosity and elusiveness of the eternal feminine. A sister to Solveig in Ibsen's *Peer Gynt* and to Indra in Strindberg's *A Dream Play*, Úa is the irresistible woman who transforms: the witch, the whore, the mother, the sexual initiator, wisdom's fount. Úa gives her age as fifty-two, which makes her twice as old as Embi—the same difference of age, she points out, as Saint Theresa and San Juan de la Cruz when *they* first met—but in fact she is a shape-shifter, immortal. Eternity in the form of a woman. Úa has been pastor Jón's wife (although she is a Roman Catholic), the madam of a brothel in Buenos Aires, a nun, and countless other identities. She appears to speak all the principal languages. She knits incessantly: mittens, she explains, for the fishermen of Peru. Perhaps most peculiarly, she has been dead, conjured into a fish, and preserved up on the glacier until a few days earlier, and has now been resurrected by pastor Jón, and is about to become Embi's lover.

This is perennial mythology, Nordic style, not just a spoof of the myth. As Strindberg put it in the preface to his forgotten masterpiece, *A Dream Play*: "Time and space do not exist." Time and space are mutable in the dream novel, the dream play. Time can always be revoked. Space is multiple.

Strindberg's timelessness and placelessness are not ironic, as they are for Laxness, who scatters a few impure details in *Under the Glacier*—historical grit that reminds the reader this is not only the folk time of Nordic mythology but also that landmark year of self-loving apocalyptic yearning: 1968. The book's author, who published his first novel when he was nineteen and wrote some sixty novels in the course of his long (he died at ninety-five) and far from provincial life, was already sixty-six years old. Born in rural Iceland, he lived in the United States in the late 1920s, mostly in Hollywood. He hung out with Brecht. He spent time in the Soviet Union in the 1930s. He had already accepted a Stalin Peace Prize (1952) and a Nobel Prize in Literature (1955). He was known for epic novels about poor Icelandic farmers. He was a writer with a conscience. He had been obtusely philo-Soviet (for decades) and was then interested in Taoism. He read Sartre's *Saint Genet* and publicly decried the American bases in Iceland and the American war on Vietnam. But *Under the Glacier* does not reflect any of these literal concerns. It is a work of supreme derision and freedom and wit. It is like nothing else Laxness ever wrote.

Comic novel.

The comic novel also relies on the naive narrator: the person of incomplete understanding, and inappropriate, indefatigable cheerfulness or optimism. Pastor Jón, Úa, the villagers: everyone tells Embi he doesn't understand. "Aren't you just a tiny bit limited, my little one?" Úa observes tenderly. To be often wrong, but never disheartened, gamely acknowledging one's mistakes, and soldiering on—this is an essentially comic situation. (The comedy of candor works best when the protagonist is young, as in Stendhal's autobiographical *La Vie de Henry Brulard*.) An earnest, innocent hero to whom preposterous things happen attempts, for the most part successfully, to take them in his stride. That the nameless narrator sometimes says "I" and sometimes speaks of himself in the third-person introduces a weird note of depersonalization, which also evokes laughter. The rollicking mixture of voices cuts through the pathos; it expresses the fragile false confidence of the comic hero.

What is comic is not being surprised at what is astonishing or absurd. The bishop's mandate—to underreact to whatever his young emissary is to encounter—sets up an essentially comic scenario. Embi always underreacts to the preposterous situations in which he finds himself: for example, the food that he is offered every day by the pastor's housekeeper during his stay—nothing but cakes.

Think of the films of Buster Keaton and Harry Langdon; think of the writings of Gertrude Stein. The basic elements of a comic situation: deadpan; repetition; defect of affectivity; deficit (apparent deficit, anyway) of understanding, of what one is doing (making the audience superior to the state of mind being represented); naively solemn behavior; inappropriate cheerfulness—all of which give the impression of childlikeness.

The comic is also cruel. This is a novel about humiliation—the humiliation of the hero. He endures frustration, sleep deprivation, food deprivation. (No, the church is not open now. No, you can't eat now. No, I don't know where the pastor is.) It is an encounter with a mysterious authority that will not reveal itself. Pastor Jón appears to have abdicated his authority by ceasing to perform the duties of a minister and choosing instead to be a mechanic, but he has actually sought access to a much larger authority—mystical, cosmic, galactic. Embi has stumbled into a community that is a coven of authority figures, whose provenance and powers he never manages to decipher. Of course they are rogues, charlatans—and they are not; or at any rate, their victims, the credulous, deserve them (as in a much darker, Hungarian novel about spiritual charlatans and rural dupes, Krasznahorkai's *Satantango*). Wherever Embi turns, he does not understand, and he is not being helped to understand. The pastor is away; the church is closed. But unlike, say, K in Kafka's *The Castle*, Embi does not suffer. For all his humiliations, he does not appear to feel anguish. The novel has always had a weird coldness. It is both cruel and merry.

Visionary novel.

The comic novel and the visionary novel also have something in common: non-explicitness. An aspect of the comic is meaninglessness and inanity, which is a great resource of comedy, and also of spirituality—at least in the Oriental (Taoist) version that attracted Laxness.

At the beginning of the novel, the young man continues for a bit to protest his inability to carry out the bishop's mission. What am I to say? he asks. What am I to do?

The bishop replies: "One should simply say and do as little as possible. Keep your eyes peeled. Talk about the weather. Ask what sort of summer they had last year, and the year before that. Say that the bishop has rheumatism. If any others have rheumatism, ask where it affects them. Don't try to put anything right. . . ."

More of the bishop's wisdom:

"Don't be personal—be dry! . . . Write in the third person as much as possible. . . . No verifying! . . . Don't forget that few people are likely to tell more than a small part of the truth: no one tells much of the truth, let alone the whole truth. . . . When people talk they reveal themselves, whether they're lying or telling the truth. . . . Remember, any lie you are told, even deliberately, is often a more significant fact than a truth told in all sincerity. Don't correct them, and don't try to interpret them either."

What is this, if not a theory of spirituality and a theory of literature?

Obviously, the spiritual goings-on at Glacier have long since left Christianity behind. (Pastor Jón holds that all the gods people worship are equally good, that is, equally defective.) Clearly, there is much more than the order of nature. But is there any role for the gods—and religion? The impudent lightness with which the deep questions are raised in *Under the Glacier* is remote from the gravitas with which they figure in Russian and in German literature. This is a novel of immense charm that flirts with being a spoof. It is a satire on religion, full of amusing New Age mumbo jumbo. It's a book of ideas, like no other Laxness ever wrote.

Laxness did not believe in the supernatural. Surely he did believe in the cruelty of life—the laughter that is all that remains of the woman, Úa, to whom Embi had surrendered himself, and who has vanished. What transpired may seem like a dream, which is to say that the quest novel concludes with the obligatory return to reality. Embi is not to escape this morose destiny.

"Your emissary crept away with his duffel bag in the middle of the laughter," Embi concludes his report to the bishop; so the novel ends. "I was a little frightened and I ran as hard as I could back the way I had come. I was hoping that I would find the main road again." *Under the Glacier* is a marvelous novel about the most ambitious questions, but since it is a novel it is also a journey that must end, leaving the reader dazzled, provoked, and, if Laxness's novel has done its job, perhaps not quite as eager as Embi to find the main road again.

Susan Sontag
New York City
December 2004

UNDER THE GLACIER

I

The Bishop
Wants an Emissary

The bishop summoned the undersigned to his presence yesterday evening. He offered me snuff. Thanks all the same, but it makes me sneeze, I said.

Bishop: Good gracious! Well I never! In the old days all young theologians took snuff.

Undersigned: Oh, I'm not much of a theologian. Hardly more than in name, really.

Bishop: I can't offer you coffee, I'm afraid, because madam is not at home. Even bishops' wives don't stay home in the evenings any more: society's going to pieces nowadays. Well now, my boy, you seem to be a nice young fellow. I've had my eye on you since last year, when you wrote up the minutes of the synod for us. It was a masterpiece, the way you got all their drivel down, word for word. We've never had a theologian who knew shorthand before. And you also know how to handle that phonograph or whatever it's called.

Undersigned: We call it a tape recorder. Phonograph is better.

Bishop: All this gramophone business nowadays, heavens above! Can you also do television? That's even more fantastic! Just like the cinema—after two minutes I'm sound asleep. Where on earth did you learn all this stuff?

Undersigned: Oh, there's nothing much to making a tape recording, really. I got some practise as a casual worker in radio. But I've never done television.

Bishop: Never mind. Tape will do us. And shorthand. It's amazing how people can learn to scribble these rats'-tails! A bit like Arabic. It's about time you got ordained! But no doubt you've got a steady job?

Undersigned: I've done some tuition in languages. And a little in arithmetic.

Bishop: I see, good at languages too!

Undersigned: Well, I've got a smattering of those five or six languages you need for matriculation; and a little bit of Spanish because I took a group of tourists to Majorca once and did some preparation for that.

Bishop: And the theology, everything all right there, is that not so?

Undersigned: I suppose so. I'm not really much of a believer, though.

Bishop: A rationalist? That's not so good! One wants to watch that sort of thing.

Undersigned: I don't know what I should be called, really. Just an ordinary silly ass, I suppose. Nothing else. I didn't do too badly in theology, though.

Bishop: Perhaps not even wanting to be ordained?

Undersigned: Haven't thought much about it.

Bishop: You ought to think about it. And then you ought to get yourself a wife. That's how it went with me. It is also wholesome to have children. That's when you first begin to understand the workings of Creation. I need someone to go on a little journey for me. If it turns out well, you will be given a good living by and by. But a wife you'll have to sort out for yourself.

I began to listen expectantly now, but the bishop began to talk about French literature. French literature is so enjoyable, he said. Don't you think so?

Undersigned: Yes, I suppose so. If one had the time for it.

Bishop: Don't you find it odd that the greatest French writers should have written books about Iceland that made them immortal? Victor Hugo wrote *Han d'Islande*, Pierre Loti wrote *Pêcheurs d'Islande*, and Jules Verne crowned it with that tremendous masterpiece about Snæfellsjökull (Snæfells Glacier), *Voyage au Centre de la Terre*. That's where Árni Saknússemm appears, the only alchemist and philosopher we've ever had in Iceland. No one can ever be the same after reading that book. Our people could never write a book like that—least of all about Snæfellsjökull.

The undersigned wasn't entirely in agreement with the bishop over the last book on the list, and declared that he himself was more impressed by that writer's account of Phileas Fogg's journey round the world than Otto Lidenbrock's descent down the crater on Snæfellsjökull.

It emerged, however, that what I thought about French literature was quite immaterial to the bishop.

Bishop: What do you say to putting your best foot forward and going to Snæfellsjökull to conduct the most important investigation at that world-famous mountain since the days of Jules Verne? I pay civil service rates.

Undersigned: Don't ask me to perform any heroic deeds. Besides, I've heard that heroic deeds are never performed on civil service rates. I'm not cut out for derring-do. But if I could deliver a letter for your Grace out at Glacier or something of that sort, that shouldn't be beyond my capacities.

Bishop: I want to send you on a three-day journey or so on my behalf. I'll be giving you a written brief for the mission. I'm going to ask you to call on the minister there, pastor Jón Prímus, for me, and tell him he is to put you up. There's something that needs investigating out there in the west.

Undersigned: What's to be investigated, if I may ask?

Bishop: We need to investigate Christianity at Glacier.

Undersigned: And how am I expected to do that—an inexperienced ignoramus like me?

Bishop: It would probably be best to begin by investigating old pastor Jón himself: for example, to establish whether the man's crazy or not, or is perhaps more brilliant than all the rest of us. He spent six years at a university in Germany trying to study history and eventually ended up as a theologian here with us. He was always a little equivocal. Some say he's lost his faith.

Undersigned: Am I to start meddling in that?

Bishop: What I want to know, because I happen to be the office boy at the Ministry of Ecclesiastical Affairs, is first of all why doesn't the man keep the church in good repair? And why doesn't he hold divine service? Why doesn't he baptise the children? Why doesn't he bury the dead? Why hasn't he drawn his stipend for ten or twenty years? Does that mean he's perhaps a better believer than the rest of us? And what does the congregation say? On three successive visitations I have instructed the old fellow to put these matters right. The office has written him all of fifty letters. And never a word in reply, of course. But you can't warn a man more than three times, let alone threaten him—the fourth time the threat just lulls him to sleep; after that there's nothing for it but summary defrocking. But where are the crimes? That's the whole point! An investigation is called for. There are some cock-and-bull stories going around just now that he has allowed a corpse to be deposited in the glacier. What corpse? It's an absolute scandal! Kindly check it! If it's a dead body, we want to lug it down to habitation and bury it in consecrated ground. And if it's something else, then what is it? The year before last I wrote to the chap who's supposed to be the parish clerk there, I've forgotten what his name is. The reply arrived yesterday, exactly eighteen months later; you can't say they're in a tearing hurry, these fellows! What sort of country bumpkins are they, may I ask? Is there some kind of mutual protection at Glacier? Against us here! Some sort of freemasonry! And this fellow's twice as crazy as pastor Jón Prímus has ever been. I think it wouldn't come amiss to examine him a little, too. Here's his bit of scribble.

The bishop handed me a dog-eared scrap of paper that could hardly have come through the post; it looked as if it had been carried from farm to farm and shuffled from pocket to pocket through many districts. Nonetheless, the letter evinced a mental attitude, if you could call it that, which has more to it than meets the eye and which expresses the logic of the place where it belongs but has little validity anywhere else, perhaps. The bishop rattled on while I ran my eye over the letter: And then he's said to have allowed anglers and foreigners to knock up some monstrosity of a building practically on top of the church—tell him from me to have it pulled down at once! Moreover, he really must get round to divorcing his wife. I've heard he's been married for more than thirty years, since long before I became bishop, and hasn't got round to divorcing his wife yet, even though it's a known fact that she has never shared bed nor board with him. Instead, he seems to have got mixed up with a woman they call Hnallþóra, of all things! Is Christianity being tampered with, or what?

Letter to the bishop from the parish clerk, one Tumi Jónsen of Brún-under-Glacier. Main contents: The writer begs indulgence for laziness with the pen, senile decay, etcetera, and is now at last getting down to answering the letter from the Bishop of Iceland, duly received the year before last, containing questions regarding Christian observance at Glacier. Likewise what truth there might be in rumours that the pastor is inadequate to his calling and that parish duties are being neglected; item, has there in recent years been any queer traffic with some unspecified casket on the glacier, and other goings-on of that nature? The parish clerk simply permits himself to place on record his unshakeable conviction that neither in this parish nor anywhere else around Glacier could anyone be found who would not acknowledge that the minister at Glacier, pastor Jón Jónsson, known as Prímus, is a man of gold. Not a living creature in this place would choose to be without pastor Jón for a single day. The whole community would be grief-stricken if a hair of his noble head were harmed. To be sure it is sometimes suggested that our pastor is not overhasty regarding his parish duties, but I venture to assert upon my conscience as parish clerk that everyone eventually gets buried with all due propriety and honour, just as in other places in the country. On the other hand, if any implement anywhere in these parts is in disrepair (because they no longer manufacture anything but rubbish here in Iceland or abroad nowadays), then you come to the crux of the matter where our pastor Jón is concerned: whatever it is that's damaged, be it utensils or machines, ladles or old knives, even broken earthenware pots, everything is resurrected as good as new or better than new at the hands of pastor Jón. I'm afraid that many a rider or motorist in these parts would think it a tragedy if pastor Jón were removed, such an excellent man to have near the main road, always ready to shoe a horse at any time of the day or night, a veritable artist at patching up people's worn-out engines so that everything goes again like new. In conclusion, it's quite true that our church is a little the worse for wear, although in fact there haven't been many complaints; but God is said to be great. No need to elaborate further on that. Your Grace's loving and obedient servant, Tumi Jónsen of Brún-under-Glacier.

2

Emissary of the Bishop: EmBi for Short

When the undersigned had eventually agreed to make the journey, the bishop said: The first thing is to have the will; the rest is technique.

The undersigned continued, for appearance's sake, to protest his youth and lack of authority to scrutinise a venerable old man's discharge of his pastoral duties or to reform Christianity in places where the words of even the bishop himself were disregarded; or what kind of "technique" could one expect from an ignorant youth in such a predicament? What am I to say? What am I to do?

Bishop: One should simply say and do as little as possible. Keep your eyes peeled. Talk about the weather. Ask what sort of summer they had last year, and the year before last. Say that the bishop has rheumatism. If any others have rheumatism, ask where it affects them. Don't try to put anything right—that's our business in the Ministry of Ecclesiastical Affairs, provided that we know what's wrong. We're asking for a report, that's all. No matter what credos or fables they come up with, you're not to try to convert them or try to reform anything or anyone. Let them talk; don't argue with them. And if they are silent, what are they silent about? Note down everything relevant—I'll give you the outline in the brief. Don't be personal—be dry! We don't want to hear anything funny from the west; we laugh at our own expense here in the south. Write in the third person as much as possible. Be academic, yes, but in moderation. Take a tip from the phonograph.

EmBi (hereinafter written Embi): If the pastor is always patching up old engines or mending saucepans and forgets to bury the dead so that corpses are taken up onto the glacier, well, can a farce be made less comical than it actually is?

Bishop: I'm asking for facts. The rest is my business.

Embi: Am I not even to say what I think about it, then?

Bishop: No no no, my dear chap. We don't care in the slightest what you think about it. We want to know what you see and hear, not how the situation strikes you. Do you imagine we're such babies here that people need to think for us and draw conclusions for us and put us on the potty?

Embi: But what if they start filling me up with lies?

Bishop: I'm paying for the tape. Just so long as they don't lie through you. One must take care not to start lying oneself!

Embi: But somehow I've got to verify what they say.

Bishop: No verifying! If people tell lies, that's as may be. If they've come up with some credo or other, so much the better! Don't forget that few people are likely to tell more than a small part of the truth: no one tells much of the truth, let alone the whole truth. Spoken words are facts in themselves, whether true or false. When people talk they reveal themselves, whether they're lying or telling the truth.

Embi: And if I find them out in a lie?

Bishop: Never speak ill of anyone in a report. Remember, any lie you are told, even deliberately, is often a more significant fact than a truth told in all sincerity. Don't correct them, and don't try to interpret them either. That's our responsibility. He who would hold his own against them, let him take care not to lose his own faith.

3

Journey from the Capital to Glacier

I travelled by bus, with my things in a duffel bag. May 11: the last day of the winter fishing season. It's the time of year called "between hay and grass," looked at from the sheep's point of view, the time when the hay has run out and the grass not yet started to grow. It's often a wearisome time for ruminants: indeed, spring has always been the season in Iceland when animals and people perish.

The few folk who are on the move at this time of year are about as commonplace as the undersigned himself; dull and nondescript; they sidle off the bus at unexpected places and vanish into the moorland beside the road as if they lived in some bog there; or else the driver pulls up at some unaccountable point in the middle of nowhere and tosses out of the window some trifle, which usually lands in a puddle: a bundle of newspapers, a small bag, a parcel.

The mountains to the right of the road are black higher up. Snowdrifts here and there, withered slopes, the broad moorlands dun-coloured between mountain and shore. But a strange sheen on the streams and lakes illumines the traveller even though the weather is murky and the errand probably not very stimulating. The sun is high at this time of year, and no darkness at night to speak of, but not yet completely light. The sheep look a little torpid still as they rummage for something in the moors; but things will soon be getting better. On the other hand the birds are sprightly enough over land and sea, they're always the first creatures to find something. The loons (great northern divers) are already on the lakes, diving underwater for lengthy periods, so they must be finding something; swans in pairs on the ponds, so white they gleam, or standing in flocks on the banks preening themselves. A tern comes flying in over the land and out to sea again.

Funny to see just the one tern, someone says; I've never seen terns except in their thousands. Then up pipes a woman, saying it was a scout sent by the other terns to see if the land was still above water.

How does she know that? someone asks.

Anyone can figure that out, says the woman, because it's only the 11th today and the tern never comes before Term-day on the 14th.

Question: Who's to say that all terns except this one come on the 14th?

Woman: It says so in the papers.

The arctic skua is a sinister bird. In a flat calm he flies like a piece of paper blowing about in a gale, hardly moving his wings at all. He lets the air do the work, and does nothing himself except steer; sometimes he pretends his flying has failed him or even that he has lost the art altogether, and he blows about and blows about until he falls with his white bottom uppermost; he starts struggling down on the ground; it's as if his wings are broken or out of joint; they trip him up when he tries to toddle, so that he almost somersaults. What's the meaning of these antics? Is it all just to tempt the ladies?

It's strange that all birds don't fly in the same way. After all, the air's just the same at the same place and the same time. I've heard that the wings of aeroplanes all conform to the same formula, whereas birds each conform to a formula of their own. It has undeniably required more than a little ingenuity to equip so many birds each with their own formula, and no expense spared, either. Nevertheless, there has perhaps never been a bird that flies as correctly as an aeroplane; yet all birds fly better than aeroplanes if they can fly at all. All birds are perhaps a little wrong, because an absolute once-and-for-all formula for a bird has never been found, just as all novels are bad because the correct formula for a novel has never been found.

4

Evening at Glacier

We are at Glacier; the driver says this is where you get off. On the seaward side of the road, behind a green hillock in the homefield, is a bare patch of gravel. On it stands a ramshackle old shed of corrugated iron, about two metres by three. It's shut. Evening; fog has settled on the brows of the mountains. Apart from the shed, the only other sign of human habitation is a decaying wooden bench of three planks, fastened to the ground beside the door. The undersigned sits down on the bench with his duffel bag beside him and brings out a map. The fog has sliced the tops off the mountains, and is thickest where the glacier should be, according to the map. There is a fine drizzle. The hillock glows green in the twilight, and lava-knuckles protrude from it here and there. When I tried the locked door again I noticed there was a board above it; some letters had been painted on it with lamp-black or tar a long time ago, and even though the lettering was blurred and grimy and the board decaying, one could still make out the words: PRIMUSES REPAIRED HERE.

The bridle path to the parsonage lay in a semicircle past the hillock. Beside the path stood a tethered calf, very wretched-looking, swollen-bellied, suffering from the scour, wry-faced, his forehead matted, hanging his head, not lowing. The visitor stops on the paving at the door. The long side of the house faced the sea, and the homefield reached to the edge of a sea-cliff where white birds sailed overhead.

Is it the bishop? a woman asks, coming to the door.

Embi: No, I'm afraid not. But I have a letter from the south.

Woman: You're the same as a bishop, and there was a telegram saying you were on the way. Do come in. But the pastor isn't at home.

It's a labyrinth of a house, put together from many elements; a long front building lying east to west, made of timber clad with corrugated iron; windows and door on the side facing the sea. Thereafter came a row of misshapen wooden hovels that merged into an infinity of turf huts, tumbledown or ruined; those farthest away had become one with the green hillocks in the homefield; this kind of architecture, one shed after the other, is a little like the propagation of coral, or cactuses. The woman invited me into the living room. Then she disappeared.

I settled down to wait. All the doors were wide open, letting in a dank draught, and the chilly bleating of the seabirds on the cliffs filled the open house in the twilight. The front door was off its hinges; the living room door opened onto the passage and creaked piercingly if one tried to move it. The room had once upon a time been painted light blue, but the paint had peeled off, leaving patches that were dark red from some even earlier coat of paint, and there were now patches on the patches; these inner patches were poison green. In the living room there was an enormously long table with wooden benches along both sides; everything was made of undressed deal planks hammered together with four-inch nails. The furniture consisted of a chest of drawers, a writing desk, and a bureau, all much the worse for wear; nor was it easy to imagine what had happened to the drawers, as they had all disappeared.

When the bishop's emissary had been sitting for an hour, he began to feel the effect of the raw cold. What was your emissary to do with himself? Should he perhaps go and look for the woman and tell her he was cold? Had he then come to a stranger's house just to complain about his own lot? He came to the conclusion that he had no right to complain. He had been sent here only to look for facts. If he had to sit here without food all night, that was as good a fact for his report as any other. It's about as unscientific as it would be dishonest to stop a scientific process in midstream on moral grounds—for instance, because one's feet are frozen.

Your emissary had occupied himself for the first hour by jotting down in shorthand an account of the day's journey, but he stopped because of the cold, besides which it was scarcely light enough to write, and that's why the journey peters out with the arctic skuas in Kolbeinsstaðir District. He gets up, stretches, wrestles with the creaking door for a bit, then goes outside and heads for the sea. He stands on the edge of the cliff—forty fathoms high in many places, at least sixty in some. These coal-black cliffs looked as if they were snow-covered, so crowded were the white birds sitting there in the dusk. On a ledge no larger than a man's palm lived many families. It is a kittiwake colony.

Even at midnight a kittiwake colony is seldom quiet at this

time of year, at least not for long. Although they all seem to
have said their prayers, suddenly someone breaks the silence in
a shrill falsetto like a fire alarm. Sometimes the voice is sharp
and pained, like the yelp of a dog wakened by its tail being
trodden on; sometimes as when an infant starts screaming in
terror out of the depths of slumber, roused by some wordless
dream that at the very worst was caused by a touch of heart-
burn. The kittiwake colony is wide awake at once and joins in
for a while, until they all agree to say their prayers again and
wait for the next reveille. The undersigned had meant to get a
little warmth into his body, but it only adds to the shivers to listen to the bleating of birds on a raw night early in spring.

5

The Story of Hnallþóra and the Fairy Ram

The time is 0000, midnight. Upon my word, isn't that some kind of coffee smell wafting towards me out of the house! Inside, the table had been covered with a cloth and laid with a variety of cakes of many shapes and colours; I think I'm safe to say that there were hundreds of them, set out on nearly twenty plates. To cap it all, the woman brought in three war-cakes, so called because they became fashionable during the war, each about twenty centimetres in diameter and about six to eight centimetres thick. Finally the woman brought in coffee and switched on the light, a naked 15-watt bulb that hung by a flex from the ceiling.

Woman, apologetically: I'm going to light this thing anyway, even though we don't go in much for that sort of thing in this house. It was forced onto pastor Jón a year or two back when every farm was connected up in accordance with the new regulations, whether people wanted to have it or not.

The undersigned wasn't very sure at first what the "this" was that couldn't be mentioned by name. Gradually it dawned on me that the woman was talking about electricity.

Embi: It's quite unnecessary to switch on the electricity for my sake. A candle will do.

Woman: That's hardly good enough for bishops.

However, the upshot was that the woman switched off the light with the unmentionable name and lit a candle; this was actually far more festive than the naked 15-watt bulb. The woman poured the visitor a cup of coffee and invited him to help himself, then took up position by the door with a stern expression on her face. The coffee had a mouldy taste, and truth to tell I was paralysed by the sight of these innumerable cakes arrayed around such awful coffee. I felt that the woman was watching over me in the same spirit of duty as when one is making sure that animals are eating the fodder they've been given.

She is a woman of dignity, but taciturn; perhaps she yearns for eternal silence and feels uncomfortable in body and soul if anyone addresses her first; it's better to tread warily. Perhaps there was just a small railing around her, like a statue in a square. A cleanly woman. Not much over sixty. Thickset, rather clumsy.

Embi: Perhaps the pastor has gone to bed?

Woman: That I do not know.

Embi: Excuse me, but aren't you the pastor's wife?

Woman: I've not been so considered hitherto.

Embi: Never before have I seen so many cakes all at once. Did you make all these cakes?

Woman: Who else, indeed? That's why they call me Hnallþóra (Pestle-Thóra) hereabouts.

Embi: An unusual name.

Miss Hnallþóra: I suppose the folk here think I wield the
pestle in the mortar rather vigorously.

Embi: A very entertaining notion, certainly.

Miss Hnallþóra: There's a lot of envy around here, you
know. The madams with their mixing machines say things
about my mortar. But what's cardamom until it's been under
the pestle, say I! Do have some more cakes.

Embi: Excuse me, but is the pastor's wife not at home
herself?

Miss Hnallþóra: I don't know. I rather think she isn't here.
Did the bishop need to have a word with her?

Embi: No, not really. I was just asking.

Miss Hnallþóra: Quite so. One could try asking down at
Neðratraðkot (Netherlane Croft). It's thought to be haunted
sometimes in springtime, or so they say.

Embi: But you're the housekeeper, are you not?

Miss Hnallþóra: I'm simply here. I go with the parsonage.

Embi: Were you already here when pastor Jón came here?

Miss Hnallþóra: Yes, I'm from up the mountain.

Embi: From up the mountain?

The lady heaved a sigh, closed her eyes, and inhaled a need-
less sort of "yes" all the way down into the lungs—yessing on
the in-breath, as it's called.

Embi: From up the mountain? Is that some particular family?

Miss Hnallþóra: I don't come from any particular family.
That's for other folk.

Embi: Nothing particular in the way of news around here?

Miss Hnallþóra: There's nothing much happens around

here. Nothing ever happens to anyone. No one has ever seen anything.

Embi: Nothing ever happened to you either? Never seen anything?

Miss Hnallþóra: Nothing to speak of.

Embi: Perhaps something you cannot speak of? Have you never owned a horse, for instance?

Miss Hnallþóra: No, praise be to God. Others have owned horses, I'm happy to say, but not me.

Embi: Who owns the calf?

Miss Hnallþóra: The calf! That thing on its last legs? I've no idea why I was given it. There's nothing here to feed to a calf except coffee once in a while, and old cakes I mash up in it. On the other hand I won't conceal the fact from anyone that once upon a time a little something happened to me. I saw a little something. But never except just that once.

Embi: This is turning out better than seemed likely.

Miss Hnallþóra: Of course, I wouldn't tell a soul about it.

Embi: That's not so good!

Miss Hnallþóra: I'll just go and make some more coffee.

Embi: Thanks, but there's really no need. I'm not accustomed to drinking more than a half a cup or so. And I'm sure that coffeepot holds at least a litre and a half.

But there was no stopping her going out again with the coffeepot to replenish it, even though the level couldn't have been lowered by much. While the lady was out, the bishop's emissary could scarcely take his eyes off the three war-cakes bulging with spices and measuring a total of sixty centimetres in diameter. I was sweating a little on the forehead.

In the hope that with a little patience some information might be got out of the lady, I accepted a third cup contrary to my custom. It worked. The visitor's coffee-swilling began to have a loosening effect on this fettered woman. Her reactions became more human, and she submitted to that softening of the soul and surrender to God and man that comes from telling a story. She returned to that one thing that had ever happened to her in her lifetime, that one and only time she had ever seen something. It was very nearly fifty years ago, but, she says, I remember it as if it had happened yesterday. May I not cut the bishop a wedge of layer cake?

Embi: There's really no need, but, well, yes, thank you.

Miss Hnallþóra: Would you not like a piece from each one? It wasn't the intention to have to throw it to the dogs.

The visitor besought her only to cut from the one, preferably the one with the sugar icing, because that one wasn't as moist as the others and wasn't oozing quite so much juice and tinned fruit. So she cut me a wedge that would have been a suitable portion for seven people, and laid it on my plate.

Miss Hnallþóra: I was just a chit of a girl at the time. I was sent on some errand out to Bervík. Instead of going the direct coastal way along the seashore, I followed the sheep-paths higher up, straight over the glacier moraines. There are lots of lovely dells up there, full of mosses and heathers. And then, as I am walking over one of the ridges, suddenly I see a brown ram with trained horns standing there on its own, with no other animal anywhere near, and looking up at me from the hollow. I've never been so frightened in all my born days, a speechless person, a helpless girl, because I knew that neither this nor any other straight-horned brown ram existed here at Glacier. A golden lustre shone from him. Never in all my born days have I seen such a fleece on any living animal. I felt I was turning to stone. For a long time I couldn't tear my eyes from this beautiful animal that I knew didn't exist here in the valley nor down by the shore nor anywhere in Iceland. The ram just stood there and gazed at me. I feel as if I'm standing there this very day and the ram is gazing at me. What was I to do? In the end I had the sense to run out of sight. I made a wide detour down from the ridge and ran helter-skelter along the hollows all the way down to the sea until I reached the main road. Thanks be to God.

Embi: A fairy ram?

The woman inhaled her answer in a falsetto, no doubt still with palpitations to this very day: I don't know.

Embi: Did anyone ever get to the bottom of this?

Miss Hnallþóra: No, of course no one ever got to the bottom of it. Everyone knew as well as I did that there were no straight-horned brown rams in these parts. Some lads from the next farm went up to have a look, but naturally they saw nothing. And since then I myself have never seen anything one could call seeing. And nothing has ever happened to me.

6

Morning at Glacier

Your emissary is up and about early. The light wasn't conducive to sleeping, especially since there was no curtain at the window of the discoloured blue room where Miss Hnallþóra had shown me to bed the previous night after the coffee; in fact it was already beginning to dawn even then.

The room was on the right-hand side of the passage from the front door, opposite the spare room. The door had only one hinge and you fastened it with a piece of string. It was evident that it had been nailed up during the winter, and would be nailed up again in the autumn.

The fog was lifting, the homefield very green after the overnight drizzle. The sheep had got into the homefield; nobody bothered to chase them out. There were a few bluebottles at the window. I felt a little queasy after the immoderate consumption of cakes and chicory-coffee. Admittedly I hadn't managed to finish even the litre and a half the woman had brought me at the first go; but what would she have expected of me if I had emptied the coffeepot twice, as she expected—three litres in all!

There was a bed in the room, certainly, but that was the only piece of furniture there: no utensils or other fittings or articles. Was it the intention that a visitor who had taken three litres of that coffee should use the bed itself, like an infant? Upon closer examination, there was in the corner a rusty washstand of the kind now much sought after by folk museums, and that I'm told are still to be found in dwellings in England. It's the kind of stand that accommodates a washbasin, ewer, and soap dish. There is some brownish water in the ewer. Has this water perhaps been used before for washing? How often? Had previous visitors used the ewer for other purposes, after drinking three litres of coffee last winter while the doors of the house were nailed up?

A ragged towel hung from a nail in the middle of the wall; it reminded one of a work of art, albeit highly abstruse, by Duchamp. It gives rise to some baffling riddles. Why is this paltry object, so frayed and tattered, given such obvious prominence that one could say it dominates the whole room? Is one to understand this shrieking towel as a gambit directed at myself—a symbol? I mustn't forget to mention that the room had been thoroughly scrubbed the day before from top to bottom, scrubbed with powerful washing soda, undoubtedly, which produced a stench of putrefaction very like the reek of cows' urine. This stink now mingled with another nasty smell, of rotting wood and musty earth from the turf wall behind the panelling. To this was added the smell of the bluebottles, curiously strong but in some way not nearly so offensive as the smell of many a vertebrate. I forgot to mention that I found it quite impossible to open the window last night before I went to bed. How these plump and powerful bluebottles had got in was a mystery to me. One thing was certain—they couldn't get out again; but perhaps that wasn't the intention, anyway. Was it conceivable that these flies had been fetched in here when the scrubbing was finished? And if so, for what purpose? Were they there as substitutes for art in the house? Or decoration? Were they there instead of goldfish or canaries? Perhaps both. Pictorial art is a delusion of the eye, whereas flies are living ornaments and much more lively than flowers, what's more, because flowers are languid in their movements and keep silent. Even goldfish are silent, but the bluebottle is the poor man's canary, endowed with a singing voice that awakens memories in the minds of visitors. The bluebottles remind the undersigned of the sunshine of childhood, but they also create moral problems that need to be resolved but that have not to my knowledge been fully resolved by moral philosophers and World Teachers. This is the dilemma I have now reached at Glacier. I ask:

1) Is it morally right to kill flies, taking all things into consideration?

2) Although it may in certain circumstances be excusable, for instance if flies are proved to be carrying disease into the house, is it still morally right for a guest to kill these creatures? Would that not be comparable to killing the host's dog?

7

Two Buildings

Your emissary has gone outside, where other tasks require attention. The fog is lifting, and there are sunshine patches on the countryside here and there. For the first time I catch a glimpse of that white tureen-lid of the world, Snæfellsjökull, between wisps of fog and the shadow of the clouds. Yesterday evening when your emissary went outside to while away the time, fog had merged with dusk and only the white birds were visible. This morning in the middle of the almost overgrown path a dandelion glistens between the paving stones and a buttercup is preparing to burst open. This is between the parsonage and the church.

And now it becomes clear that there was something in what the bishop had said when he warned his emissary that a monstrosity had been built in the west: at any rate, the church looks

somewhat insignificant beside this edifice. For one thing, they
hadn't even managed to put this monster parallel to the church,
but at an angle to it. Either the people who built it hadn't noticed
that a church was there, or else they had wanted to trample on the
church's toes: there is only just enough space for a person to
squeeze between this building and the church.

Suffice it to say meantime that the church is built of timber
and had originally been clad with corrugated iron, but there's
only the odd sheet of it left on the walls here and there. I also
note *pro tem* that the church seems only moderately suited to
attracting a congregation. Windows boarded with boxwood,
the main door securely nailed shut. The churchyard looks in
sad condition, too; not a single cross at a proper angle to its
foundation any longer; these memorials, some made of rusty
iron, others of rotten wood, all look decidedly tipsy. Withered
grass stands between the graves higher than I have ever seen
elsewhere. On the other hand, the birdsong is in good heart,
with the thrush's trilling whistle from the church gable and the
soughing bleat of seabirds from the nearby cliffs.

We turn now from this poor House of Glory to the edifice
already mentioned. Timber structures of this kind are called
bungalows, from whatever language that might be and whatever it might mean. Usually this word applies to a single-storey
country cottage that wealthy white men in the colonies built
for themselves to ape the native style of architecture, except
that it's made of choicest wood and equipped with all modern
luxuries.

Half in a dream, your emissary went over to this model of
avant-garde architecture in a homefield where the entire hus-
bandry consisted of one ailing calf.

No road led to this building from any direction, not even a path. Windows carefully shuttered, with nowhere a chink for a Peeping Tom. On the south and west sides were broad covered verandas, presumably to provide shade from the sun. Everything closed and locked.

8

Interrogation of the Parish Clerk

Your emissary happened to glance into the living room and saw that many goodly cakes were on the scene again, this time intended for breakfast, as well as the three war-cakes from the evening before. I presumed that the mighty coffeepot would soon be making its appearance, so I sneaked out again backwards, taking care not to touch that noisily creaking door.

On the map of the district the parish clerk's farm, Brún, is indicated at the roots of the mountain about two or three kilometres away. It would be advisable to have a talk with the clerk before pastor Jón returns from his travels.

A farmer gave me a lift in his jeep and took me some of the way. The man asked if your emissary was on a holiday outing, and I said yes. But isn't it very boring, tramping the highway on foot like this, the man asked. I said no. Once one starts telling lies it's difficult to start telling the truth again. Had I said I had been sent by the Ministry of Ecclesiastical Affairs or by the bishop, I would have been thought rather a dangerous creature. Country people cannot understand why the emissaries of Christendom don't drive about in cars; indeed, it's unlikely that Saint Paul would have been flogged in Thessalonica if he had had a jeep in working order.

The farm is a sort of longhouse on the same coral-principle as the parsonage. It doesn't look as if it has been cared for much this century, except that a concrete porch with steep cement steps has been built onto the old timber house, and this remarkable structure protrudes from the middle of the side-wall. Perhaps someone once had the idea of entering the house at some other point than through the front door, wherever that might have been originally. It must have been quite a job to build such an excrescence onto a wooden house clad with corrugated iron. The gravel used for the concrete was too coarse, and there was too much sand in proportion to the cement, with probably quite a lot of clay or even soil in the sand, because the concrete is all cracked and there is grass growing in the fissures, as well as some sorrel and the little white flowering chickweed called alpine mouse-ear. Soon this porch will be reduced to a pile of rubble on the paving, and then there will be a hole left in this turn-of-the-century house.

The farmer left his work and invited me inside after I had explained who I was.

Embi: Are you Tumi Jónsen, clerk of the congregation?

Farmer: So they say. I'm only passing on what I've been told.

Embi: Are you Danish?

Farmer: No such luck, I fear. I am directly descended from those famous Jónsens who wrote the History of Iceland.

Tumi Jónsen is well over sixty, perhaps seventy or eighty, his features marked by toil and kindliness. His bald pate is the colour of parchment, but the eyebrows are fair, the eyes blue and a little rheumy. He asks the news from the south, and then if the roads aren't more passable now. Then: Is everything going well with our bishop, the blessed creature?

Embi: Yes, thank you, although he has a touch of rheumatism. I am to give you his greetings, and his thanks for the letter. He asked me to inquire if you are troubled with rheumatism?

Tumi Jónsen: The dear light of heaven! That's just like him. He is a noble soul. Are you in orders, may I ask?

Embi: No, just an errand-boy.

Tumi Jónsen: It is nice to be modest, my boy. Please take a seat. But the womenfolk aren't at home, I fear; they went into town to buy some soap. They say that spring is here. Time to start scrubbing. I hope they will be back soon to make the coffee.

The parish clerk opened his trunk and brought out a bottle of port and one beaker; he filled the glass and drained it and said: I'm drinking first, because I am the older. But had you been in orders, I would have let you drink first.

He wiped the inside of the glass with his thumb, filled it again, and handed it to me in silence. Then he put the bottle and beaker back in the trunk and closed it.

Embi: So you are the parish clerk?

Tumi Jónsen: You can put a name to anything, my boy.

Embi: Yes, well, I hardly know how to raise the subject. I'm only twenty-five years old. I haven't the faintest idea about the cure of souls. I cannot imagine how I've blundered into this.

Tumi Jónsen: Perhaps I could fill your glass again?

Embi: No thanks, I'm sweating enough already. I am wondering why the pastor isn't at home. Gone abroad, perhaps?

Tumi Jónsen: No, I hardly imagine our pastor Jón's gone

there. I imagine he was fetched over to Nes late yesterday to shoe a herd of horses. It must have taken them all night.

Embi: I thought he mended primus stoves?

Tumi Jónsen: He can do everything, that man. But primus stoves have for the most part gone into disuse since the electricity came.

Embi: Are there no electric primus stoves?

Tumi Jónsen: Not that I have heard of.

Embi: What are primus stoves, exactly? What's a primus like?

Tumi Jónsen: A primus, let me put it this way, has a head on it that is heated by burning meths. The oil is pumped from the container into the red-hot head, you light a match, and then a gas is formed that starts burning. A blue flame. Yes, that's the way of it. These contraptions replaced the old oil stoves in their day.

Embi: And a lot of people here have primus stoves in disrepair, would you say?

Tumi Jónsen: That is perhaps putting it too strongly. They're a lot of bother; and besides, the electricity is here. But I wouldn't swear to it that pastor Jón hasn't got a primus himself. Nowadays he does mostly electrical repairs—for other people, that's to say, because he doesn't use the electricity himself.

Embi: Are there any grounds for thinking that he sometimes overlooks his pastoral duties, like for example burying the dead and suchlike?

Tumi Jónsen: Some people claim he's none too quick at burying.

Embi: But everyone's satisfied?

Tumi Jónsen: True enough, it can be a little inconvenient for those who don't need burying. It matters less for the others. On the other hand he's the only person hereabouts who can shoe a horse properly. I don't think there's a single horse in these parts that pastor Jón hasn't stuck a shoe on.

Embi: So it doesn't matter if burying gets forgotten?

Tumi Jónsen: Some people find it a little odd, perhaps. But so far as I know, everyone gets to the right place in the end.

Embi: And his doctrine's all right?

Tumi Jónsen: Well, now, there's no fear of our pastor Jón saying more than he should.

Embi: What does he lay most emphasis on in his doctrine?

Tumi Jónsen: We've never been aware that pastor Jón had any particular doctrine, and we like it that way.

Embi: What does he preach, then?

Tumi Jónsen: Large questions often get little answers, my boy. Pastor Jón did not preach much in the past and preaches even less now—fortunately, many people would say. But it's not that we here are against doctrines, least of all if there's no need to follow them. Doctrines are for entertainment, I've always felt. In a parish not far from here there's a pastor who has preached a lot. People have started to take what he said seriously. It has not turned out well. People tend to do the opposite of what they are taught.

Embi: Many unbaptised children in the parish?

Tumi Jónsen: I haven't counted them.

Embi: But don't you find it tiresome, all the same?

Tumi Jónsen: Some people find it a little odd, perhaps; but the children thrive.

Embi: I want to put a question to you now as parish clerk: have you any plans in hand concerning God's House in the parish?

Tumi Jónsen: The church? Oh, dear, so you went and had a look at that too, my boy!

Embi: The church is nailed up.

Tumi Jónsen: Well now, what a shame, the church nailed up! Yes, you are right, the hinges really do need mending. And panes needed for the windows, what's more. That is not so good. A lot of good visitors come here in the summer to have a look around. And then it is bad if the church is nailed up.

Embi: What does the congregation itself think? Don't they think it bad that the church cannot be opened?

Tumi Jónsen: Oh, I wouldn't say that.

Embi: At Christmas, for example?

Tumi Jónsen: There are so many entertainments nowadays.

Embi: Perhaps there isn't even a service at Christmas?

Tumi Jónsen: No special services at Christmas, no, one can't really say that.

Embi: I wonder who broke the windowpanes in the church?

Tumi Jónsen: Oh, just some practical jokers, I expect; unprincipled youths from other districts. They could also have gone in a storm, the wretched panes. It can be pretty gusty here at Glacier, my boy.

9

Women Bring Soap

A jeep came roaring onto the paving outside the window: a cracked silencer, or no exhaust pipe. The women climbed out with the soap. The older woman had that drained, tolerant look that was for a long time the net profit that older country people earned from life's struggle; the other was in good shape, at least twenty-five to thirty years younger, wearing a floral print dress. The parish clerk introduced the women from the window.

Tumi Jónsen: There is my dear wife, if I may speak so ill of any human being. The other is our stepdaughter, Jósefína. She brings us the spring from the south with her scrubbing brush. It is she who does all the cleaning for everybody.

Stepmother and stepdaughter came in by the kitchen door, and the business of introduction continued.

Tumi Jónsen: The visitor whom you for your part see here, my dear girls, well, he is not actually the bishop of Iceland, but the same as. To be the same as—that to my mind is the same as being more than the bishop. Such a man is at once what the bishop is and in addition what he himself is: a nice young man.

The housewife offered the visitor a limp, rather clammy hand, without change of expression; after all these years she had doubtless long since given up heeding the things her husband went on about. The floral stepdaughter, for her part, had a meaty palm with a firm thumb muscle, and gave her name as she greeted him, as they do in the south: Mrs. Fína Jónsen, widow, from Hafnarfjörður. The coffee will be ready at once. And plenty of Prince Polo biscuits.

Tumi Jónsen: Yes, there's a lot in the papers about extravagance nowadays. Prince Polo biscuits are what we have indulged in here since prosperity came to the land. Perhaps those who write in the papers don't have Prince Polo biscuits.

The undersigned declined the offer of coffee and Prince Polo biscuits even though the latter might be the Icelander's present-day mark of prosperity. But it isn't the custom in the country to take it seriously if people decline coffee and cakes; and Mrs. Fína Jónsen went out to put the kettle on. She didn't close the door behind her, but carried on chatting while she busied herself.

Mrs. Fína Jónsen: Well then, I've heard the Angler's back on the rivers now. There's gold on the go! Let's hope the sea trout's running. Yes, what a man! But we'll carry on scrubbing our kitchen ceiling, mother, as if nothing's happened.

The widow started to prepare her soap-water in a tub at the kitchen door, and went on talking from out of the tub: Do you make anything by tramping round the country for bishops, young man?

Embi: Not a great deal, no, madam.

Mrs. Fína Jónsen: What are these bishops really for, when they don't make anything by it? And these professors? It said in the *Vísir* newspaper the other day that washerwomen make much more than bishops and professors.

Embi: That's probably not far off the mark.

Tumi Jónsen: Yes, it's no joke.

Mrs. Fína Jónsen: Obviously it's for no other reason than that they get neither hourly rates nor overtime. Get up on this chair, mother, and clear the shelves while I'm preparing the soap-water. Yes, just imagine it: the Angler's back! Who knows, we might get the fishing lodge to do at hourly rates tonight!

Mrs. Fína Jónsen was still bending over her tub mixing the soap-water at the open door. If your emissary had not been a guest in the house he would have closed the door between kitchen and living room, since he had no desire to gaze too long at the woman's rump and thighs as she bent over double. He got to his feet and said thank you for the welcome and made ready to take his leave. In confidence to the parish clerk: As you can see, sir, I am rather inexperienced. I don't fathom much of all this, to be honest. Perhaps I could see you again when I've had a word with pastor Jón, if not tomorrow then the day after. But there was one little question on the tip of my tongue just now, perhaps two . . .

Tumi Jónsen: Go ahead, my boy, ask anything you like. There is no harm in asking questions. But many would say you could not find a more useless respondent at Glacier than Tumi Jónsen.

Embi: First question—is there any truth in the story that a mysterious casket was taken onto the glacier a few years ago?

The parish clerk scratched himself under the collar with a finger: Fína, dear, have you heard anything about that?

Mrs. Fína Jónsen: Heard about what?

Parish clerk: That something was taken onto the glacier?

Mrs. Fína Jónsen: How should I know? The nonsense one hears!

Housewife, also from the kitchen: Has pastor Jón had anything to say about it?

Parish clerk: It depends on what the bishop thinks.

Embi: In your letter to the bishop there is a reference to "queer traffic with some unspecified casket on the glacier," without any explanation.

Parish clerk: I could not restrain myself from mentioning it in the letter as unbecoming gossip.

Embi: Before I talk to pastor Jón I would rather have something more to go on than gossip. By the way, what is gossip? Is gossip timely or untimely talk about events that have verifiably taken place? Or is it an out-and-out lie?

Housewife, mumbling in the kitchen in a rather slow, deep drawl, always on the same note: Could it not be either and both? On the other hand, as the old people used to say, truth should often be left alone. The wild horses and the snow buntings should know best the kind of man pastor Jón is; indeed, these creatures follow him around in droves. Even the ravens join company with him if they see him out in the open; and that I like less, because they have been seen to do wicked things, ravens.

Mrs. Fína Jónsen, up on the kitchen bench with her floral dress hitched up, having started to scrub the ceiling: I could well believe there are gold coins in that casket. Let's just hope it isn't a woman.

Embi: Is it possible that anyone here knows the name and address of anyone who knows the facts of the matter?

Mrs. Fína Jónsen: You could try asking Jódínus. That devil must have got his hoard of gold from somewhere or other.

Embi: Jódínus? Whose son is he, and where does he live?

Mrs. Fína Jónsen: Jódínus Álfberg, whose son is he? It's never occurred to me that he had any particular father. He's just a twelve-tonner darling. And a poet. As if I haven't tried to get out of him what's in the casket! If you tell him I sent you, he'll kill me. Mother, the kettle's boiling over. Who knows, the Angler might have an idea, if anyone had the nerve to ask him.

Embi: Who is this angler?

Mrs. Fína Jónsen stepped from her lofty perch and smoothed down her print dress: A bishop or the same as, and hasn't heard of the Angler! It was he who hooked the forty-pound salmon in the river Bláfeldará and lost it. The fish broke the rod. What people do you bishops know?

Embi: Lost the big one, eh? The biggest fish get away at times. But it is often difficult to prove it.

Mrs. Fína Jónsen: But the Angler hooked his fish again the same day. No one believed he had lost such a big salmon. But that evening the fish manifested itself. They found it again at the mouth of the river with the rod and everything in its jaws. Forty pounds. There has never been another man like him in Iceland. Nor such a fish. Or the women he has around him, imagine it! It's said he's got a wife in I don't remember how many capital cities. But the most fantastic was the one he hooked here at Glacier.

Embi: What female was that?

Mrs. Fína Jónsen: It was one of those with exceptional flesh hereabouts.

Embi: And what happened?

Mrs. Fína Jónsen: One could try asking pastor Jón.

Parish clerk: I fear you have not got the story absolutely right there, Fína dear. On the other hand it is quite true that a famous man built a fishing lodge practically under pastor Jón's nose.

Mrs. Fína Jónsen: I was married in Hafnarfjörður for ten years, daddy. In Hafnarfjörður one can tell the truth to anyone at all. It's not like here. For whom do you think the Angler built a fishing lodge almost on top of pastor Jón? No sooner had it been built than the woman disappeared—but that's another story. Dead. Everyone knows that. But the salmon came back, all right.

Embi: You mentioned exceptional flesh earlier, madam. I'm sorry, I wasn't quite clear whether you were referring to a human being or a salmon. It needs explaining. One talks of exceptional fish or exceptional meat, but I've never heard tell of exceptional flesh. What's the yardstick?

Mrs. Fína Jónsen: Well, for example, take my flesh—that's inferior and coarse flesh. No one wants that sort of flesh, any more than carrion. Nor indeed has anyone ever built a fishing lodge for it. I suppose it would be that wretch Jódínus, if anyone ever did.

Embi: You were nonetheless married to a man in Hafnarfjördur for ten years, according to your own account.

Mrs. Fína Jónsen: Yes, my late husband, he was a lovely, darling man, God knows. But he wasn't the world's greatest angler.

The mother, from the kitchen: No need to overdo it!

Mrs. Fína Jónsen: Not even a twelve-tonner man like Jódínus. On the other hand, I was good enough for my man even though I've always had rather poor flesh and my hide isn't very good, and I'm not flawless inside.

Embi: Was he a whaler?

Mrs. Fína Jónsen: He wasn't even a shark fisherman. But

though he didn't catch much he had a lively interest in fish. He was the only person in the whole country who listened to the herring news on the radio and kept up with the bankruptcies of the quick-freezing plants. And he took a pinch of snuff occasionally. Went out and bought *Vísir*. And so on. But it was I who owned the scrubbing brush.

10

Doughty Women at Glacier

I t's appropriate here to make a long story short.

Your emissary, however, doesn't wish to delay giving a summary of the tales that have lived here in this part of the land since time immemorial about a mysterious woman: sometimes one, sometimes a multitude. Sometimes this woman has taken the form of some rather disagreeable luggage.* Tumi Jónsen has now started to tell the Icelandic sagas in a style that consists principally of casting doubt on the story being told, making no effort to describe things, skating past the main points, excusing the main characters for performing deeds that will live as long as the world endures, erasing their faces if possible—but wip-

---

* The woman, named Þórgunna in the thirteenth-century *Eyrbyggja Saga*, caused great trouble when her dead body was being transported from Snæfellsnes to the bishopric at Skálholt.

ing them clean, just in case. Therefore it never becomes a story, at best just a subject for a poem. The women carry on with their scrubbing. This was a long morning.

The first woman of the district, that Þórgunna who came here from Dublin in days of yore, was a mystery woman who was the origin of the Fróðá Marvels in the days of *Eyrbyggja Saga*. Þórgunna was tall in stature and magnificently buxom, always sumptuously attired, says Tumi, and the most doughty of women though she was nearly fifty; in those days, women were called doughty who nowadays would be called exceptional. It is not quite clear from the old books what nationality Þórgunna was, whether Scottish, Cimbrian, Celtic, or Irish, except that she wasn't Nordic. It is therefore not likely that her name was Þórgunna. What her real name was we do not know, on the other hand, says Tumi Jónsen. One thing is certain, though— she caused more uncanny happenings at Glacier than most other women.

This woman was particularly skilled at using runes, and stories of her supernatural power are still an important subject for research by historians, although many find it rather a sensitive matter. The woman caused the death of nineteen men on land and sea, and raised them all from the dead to attend their own funeral feasts. Those who had been drowned at sea sat down by the fire dripping wet and started wringing themselves dry, but those who had been buried in cairns shook out their clothes and spattered everyone with earth. It could be, of course, says Tumi Jónsen, that they were simply practical jokers, youths from another district, perhaps, who had disguised themselves in order to play a trick on people. When the woman died she was laid in a travel-trunk she owned, as portmanteaux used to be called in the old days. She had been a Christian, and this

happened in the year 1000. At her own request she was transported for burial to Skálholt, because then there was no other
churchyard in the land except that one alone. Þórgunna was
buried there, the first person in consecrated ground of whom
stories tell. But some scholars reckon that this churchyard was
not established until a good fifty years later, says Tumi Jónsen.

From Glacier it takes five days to travel to Skálholt. The pallbearers had a strenuous journey with their burden over mountain ranges and fast-flowing rivers, and were often in a bad way.
Icelanders are not particularly hospitable in the sagas, and that
reputation persisted for a long time, although things have
improved since coffee was discovered; the farmers made no effort
to ease the journey for those who were carrying a Christian
corpse about the country. At Neðranes in Stafholtstungur they
were even refused food, but were allowed to sleep in the spare
room and keep the corpse in an outhouse. But during the night
the woman's huge corpse rose to its feet stark naked, went to
the pantry and fetched flour, and then went to the kitchen and
baked for her pallbearers bread in the Irish style and gave them
thick slices from the loaf.

In explanation of this phenomenon the storyteller, Tumi
Jónsen, has this to say: It could be, however, that it was actually
flatbread. Flatbread is thought to have been more common in
those days than bread in loaves. Some have argued that the
foregoing incident happened to the pallbearers in their dreams.
Others reckon that the men were deluded and that some other
woman than Þórgunna was involved. My ancestors, the Jónsens,
believed everything in the Icelandic sagas and I go along with
them sort of more or less, though I am not the man my father
and my forefathers were.

11

The Story of Úrsalei

The bishop's emissary now put question number two to the parish clerk as follows:

Question No. 2: Is there any truth in the story that pastor Jón Prímus got married in his younger days, but that his wife ran away from him and that the pastor has since then taken no steps to obtain a lawful divorce from her?

Tumi Jónsen's reply according to the emissary's shorthand (unnecessary wordiness omitted):

The story goes that a woman came to Iceland, some say from England, others from Ireland or even Spain, who was called Úrsúla the English, or Úrsa, known as Úrsalei-at-Glacier. This happened in the days of the merchant Þorleifur *ríki* (the Powerful) of Stapi, the son of Árni, farmer and sheriff of Reykjavík, the son of Ingibjörg, the daughter of Narfi of Narfeyri. Some say that on one of his business trips to Scotland, the said Þorleifur had seduced this highborn maiden of noble English and Spanish lineage and brought her to Iceland with him, to Glacier. I would not dare to vouch for the truth of this story, but I do not dispute the accepted view that Úrsalei was certainly an Irish-Spanish noblewoman of carefully selected stock on both sides for many generations in the matter of flesh, and that she was therefore a thoroughbred. On the male side, all but a select few were said to have been castrated, and the story goes on to say that female children of this clan were suckled by wet nurses until they reached marriageable age. I'm only passing on what I've been told. But reliable scholars have asserted on their conscience that the fleshly conditions in Úrsalei's family were such that those ladies can best be likened to the women the newspapers nowadays call "bombs," named after powder-filled canisters designed to cause an explosion.

Another "tradition" in which Tumi Jónsen says he has as much faith as the first one: Úrsalei early got an urge, considered by scholars to be quite rare among the aristocracy, in that she had a burning desire to become a ship's stewardess. This was granted her. On one of her journeys she landed in Iceland, at Glacier. Some might find this a little strange. Not to make a long story of it—no sooner had Úrsalei stepped ashore at Stapi than the Glacier men set to with all their celebrated broadmindedness and, saving your presence, gave the girl a baby. None can escape from destiny. For that reason Úrsúla the English settled here in these parts, according to this version of the story. The Annals say she later married the merchant Þorleifur *ríki* of Stapi. Her name, unfortunately, has never been found in the parish registers, but there was a needy anchoress of that name living in a hovel near Búðir in the seventeenth century. The world's unsure and the earth is dung, as it says in the verse. And

though I counsel people to believe the Annals only in moderation, there is no doubt that a strange woman has propagated
her breed in these parts; her descendants are alive to this day. A
host of place-names in the district are associated with her, and
always the loveliest places.

Mrs. Fína Jónsen sings:

> *Úrsúlabrow and Úrsúlalock*
> *Úrsúlatoe and Úrsúlasock*
> *Úrsúlagully and Úrsúladock*
> *Everything under the sun's in hock.*

Embi: What poetry is that, madam?

Mrs. Fína Jónsen: It's a nursery rhyme from Glacier. All to
do with Úrsúla the English. This is her realm, although no one
in Hafnarfjörður knows of her.

Embi: Nor in the bishop's office, either. And I'm afraid
there's not much chance that this intelligence will be of much
use to us there in the immediate future.

I glance through my notes and summarise: Inquired about
the church and parish life; answer—about the feeding of snow
buntings and the shoeing of horses. Inquired about suspicious
journeys, possibly funerals, up on the glacier; answer—about a
corpse that rose up naked and baked bread for its pallbearers.
Regarding the parish pastor's marital status, I get news of a
Spanish noblewoman who was suckled all her life until the
Glacier men gave her a baby. Instructive replies, but rather tan-
gential to the questions I was trying to raise. Could be a little
difficult for the people in the Ministry of Ecclesiastical Affairs
to make head or tail of information of this kind.

Tumi Jónsen: On the whole, there are various things at Glacier that people would find difficult to understand if understanding of the womenfolk is lacking.

Embi: If these women have no human characteristics, there's a risk they will not throw much light on things in my report.

Mrs. Fína Jónsen: It's said of Úrsúla the English and these women, and no doubt applies to Þórgunna as well, that they never wash.

Embi begins to get bored with all this: Haven't they got smelly armpits, then?

Mrs. Fína Jónsen: Always clean. The cleanest women at Glacier. Never seen to eat, but always plump. No one's seen them sleep, but ready for anything, even at three in the morning. Never known to read a book, but never stumped by anyone, however learned. Oddest of all, though, they never age. They disappear one fine day like birds, but never decline; always as doughty as Þórgunna; even come back from the grave as ghosts.

Tumi Jónsen: They've been known to make rather poor wives; not easy to cope with, despite that good flesh. Could be that their husbands did not always have the qualities that suited such women.

Mrs. Fína Jónsen: Everyone in the know is agreed that they have exceedingly beautiful navels.

Postscript: It's a dangerous mission for Lapps, said Ingimundur the Old's Finns in *Vatnsdœla Saga*, when he sent them on a magic journey to explore Iceland. One poor little part-time tutor from the south has no motorway to guide him when he finds himself in the footsteps of the extraordinary Otto Lidenbrock, who years ago went looking for the Icelander Árni Saknússemm. Professor Lidenbrock followed the trail of this philosopher and alchemist down the crater on Snæfellsjökull all the way to the centre of the earth; there he found Saknússemm's rusty old knife lying on the bare ground. I seem to recall that Professor Lidenbrock came out again through Stromboli. Perhaps the poor part-time tutor who writes this has yet to go through the centre of the earth before Christianity at Glacier is fully explored. But where shall I come up?

12

Farriers

The sun shone on the glacier and the door of the primus repair shop was wide open. Horses were shod here, too. On the 18th of June, 1857, when professor Dr. Otto Lidenbrock came here, the parish pastor had been busy shoeing a horse; and it's the same today, but this time with a helper. The horse was tethered to the staple on the door of the shed. The farrier took after his predecessor and finished shoeing the horse before greeting any visitors. The horse was a big rawboned beast, not properly moulted yet and not in good condition after the winter. A farm-owner stood with his back under the horse with its hock in his arms, holding up the hoof for the shoe; the farrier was fastening it, wearing smithy clothes, his hair grey-streaked and dishevelled. He had the shoe-nails in his mouth. This big horse would certainly have had no difficulty in wrenching the staple from the door-frame or even yanking the shed from its base.

Farrier: May I ask the visitor to hold the horse for a moment just while I'm finishing? We didn't have the heart to put a muzzle-noose on him. It wouldn't do any harm to scratch him behind the ears. Unfortunately I don't have a horse-scratcher.

The undersigned caught hold of the horse's reins at the muzzle and began to scratch him behind the ear. The horse accepted this and quietened down, so the undersigned began to contemplate the glacier. In actual fact the glacier is too simple a sight to appertain to what is called beautiful, which no one knows the meaning of and by which everyone means something different from everyone else: one of those words it is safer to not use about a glacier nor anything else.

The undersigned has never before seen this mountain glacier except from too far away, but was now about to become acquainted with it for a while. The mountain reminds one of an upturned earthenware bowl, the glazing a little bluish at times, but sometimes like gold-rimmed transparent Chinese porcelain, especially if the sun is low in the west over the sea, because then the rays play on the glacier from two directions. From here the glacier looks somewhat coarse-grained like a print that isn't good enough; the ice is rain-sullied in many places in the lower regions, and has developed streaks like a smudged print. Probably half the snowdrifts on the glacier have yet to melt before one can say that summer has arrived. Some magnetism that I cannot yet explain draws one's eyes towards the summit. There is a hollow on the summit, and two brilliantly white glacial crests rear upwards, bathed in an icy mesmerising light. Between these crests lies the crater into which, on the advice of the alchemist Árni Saknússemm, the party of three plunged—Professor Lidenbrock from Hamburg and his kinsman Axel, and the Icelander Hans Bjelke talking out of some dictionary or other that appears to have existed in France in the middle of the nineteenth century and could have been Swedish; and these fellows found the centre of the earth, as has been mentioned.

Pastor Jón Prímus has finished shoeing. He straightens up, rubs his palms together to clean them, comes over to me and greets me: a tall, slim, sinewy man, begrimed with iron filings, rust, smithy soot, and lubricating oil. Through all this in-grained dirt twinkles a pair of lively eyes, blue as springwater in sunshine.

Pastor Jón Prímus: What a way to treat visitors at Glacier—making them scratch a horse! It's a shame I haven't managed to get a decent horse-scratcher from Reykjavík, though I've tried for long enough. They've got nothing but plain cow-scratchers.

The undersigned reached into his pocket and brought out the bishop's written brief. Pastor Jón Prímus put on a pair of seamstress spectacles and read it. The letter was quite short.

Pastor Jón Prímus: I was hoping the bishop would be coming himself. He's a terribly agreeable chap. I always find it so enjoyable to blether with the old fellow. We don't agree about anything. But everything depends on agreeing to disagree. I hope his rheumatism is better. But I don't rightly know what I'm to make of you. What is your status, if I may ask?

Embi: I tutor in arithmetic and Danish.

Pastor Jón Prímus: I want you make the acquaintance of an eminent out-parishioner from a distant county who has come here in search of two stray horses, one red, the other grey. He has found the grey one and got news of the red one. He is my good friend Helgi of Torfhvalastaðir in Langavatnsdalur, the district officer for his area. He owns the biggest horses in the country. Do come and greet the bishop's emissary, Helgi.

Helgi of Torfhvalastaðir is a ruddy, red-haired man with a large honest face and a powerful gleam in his glasses; he came toward me with a sunny smile straight from outer space and said in a thin silky voice through the smile: I have always had a weakness for buying big horses. What a pleasure it would be now if one could debate with learned men and not have to go and look for horses!

Pastor Jón: There will be plenty of time to debate with bishops, my dear Helgi, when you have found the red one.

Helgi of Torfhvalastaðir in Langavatnsdalur (hereinafter called the Langvetningur in the text): It so happens that I have promised both the nags for a glacier trip tomorrow morning.

Pastor Jón: I shall shoe the red one for you as well when you bring him in. But that's all you're getting from me. The other matter we were discussing we shan't mention again, my friend; we shall agree to disagree on that, and be just as good friends in spite of it.

Langvetningur: Well, I don't need to rely on you any more, my dear pastor Jón. Now I can ask the bishop himself, who happens to be here with us, I understand, *per analogiam*. But while I remember, pastor Jón, what do I owe you for the shoeing?

Pastor Jón: Let us say 25 aurar the foot *per analogiam*, since you brought the shoes yourself.

Langvetningur: It's said they have stopped minting 25-aurar pieces, pastor Jón.

Pastor Jón: Well, come back anyway when you have found the red one.

Langvetningur, perhaps to me, since he had argued it many a time with the pastor: As a matter of fact, we're making a trip up the glacier to fetch a little something tomorrow morning, and it could well be that we shall need the church.

Pastor Jón: You had better be getting on your way now, old chap, and lead not the devil into temptation, as the late pastor Jens of Setberg used to say to people.

13

A Highly Responsible Office

Pastor Jón: Please excuse him for not using Latin in the right places. He is a unique person in this world. But he must not be allowed to know it. He has a theory; or more accurately, a fable. He thinks he has discovered the powder. I hope he keeps it dry. But when he says he needs the use of a church, then I say Pass and nothing will shift me from that.

Embi: What does he want with a church?

Pastor Jón: They are going to attempt reanimation there.

Embi: I'm sorry, I'm rather out of my depth.

Pastor Jón: The idea is to receive omnipotence from the galaxies. Snæfellsjökull is said to have communion. That's all to the good. But the church they shall not get—not with my permission. Besides, it's nailed shut.

Embi: That reminds me, pastor Jón. Nailed shut? The church!

That's rather sad news. Who nailed this church shut? What can be done?

Pastor Jón: The glacier stands open.

Embi: Someone said there had been no divine service at Christmas. Is that true?

Pastor Jón: That which is beyond words remains silent at Christmas too, my friend. But the glacier is there, all right.

Embi: The bishop has sent me to offer assistance in solving the problems he thinks this congregation is facing.

Pastor Jón: Few people realise the responsibility that is placed on the man who has to see to Christianity at Glacier. It is no easy matter. I was shoeing a herd of out-parish horses all night. Many people criticise me for giving hay-sweepings to alien free-range horses and shoeing out-parish herds. I ask—what is an out-parish herd and what is an in-parish herd?

Embi: The living requirements of horses—are they so pressing that the cure of souls has to take second place?

Pastor Jón: We know only one thing for certain about a horse: it belongs to no church parish, not baptised, not redeemed, with a drunk man on its back. And moreover, no need for it in the land now that both the drunk and the sober are driving machines. And yet people go on owning this creature to brag about it, torture it, write eulogies about it, and eat it. But it's not enough just to torture horses and eulogise them as they do here: they have to be shod so that they can be driven to the slaughterhouse. I regard the shoeing of horses as pertaining to the cure of souls. But the church they shall not get, not even for horses.

Embi: Perhaps the horse-owners aren't the same as those who want communion with the galaxies?

Pastor Jón: Yes, they are the same people.

Embi: The bishop is gravely concerned about this situation. What can we do for you?

Pastor Jón: Would you like to muck out the byre for me?

Embi: It's not actually in the brief. On the other hand, I was taught that there is no difference of degree in work, only in workmanship.

Pastor Jón Prímus laughs like a little boy who is posing riddles for grown-ups but despises their sagacity because he knows the answers himself: I have no cow, you see. Got rid of cows long ago. But now Hnallþóra's been given a calf.

Embi: This calf met the undersigned on arrival last night.

Pastor Jón: Didn't you think he looks rather philosophical? Hnallþóra thinks he'll die. I think he'll live. Spring is on the side of calves.

Embi: In a way, a good representative.

Pastor Jón: Certainly closer to the Creation of the world than the parish pastor.

Embi: I don't doubt that a calf fulfils his role in the Creation of the world even if he's dying of starvation. The parish pastor, on the other hand, has the role of preaching to farmers. Why does he not fulfil that role?

Pastor Jón: Farmers have cattle and kinsfolk.

Embi: Cattle die, kinsfolk die.

Pastor Jón: It doesn't matter.

Embi: We ourselves must also die.

Pastor Jón: Allah is Allah.

Embi: No revelation?

Pastor Jón: The lilies of the field.

Embi: Yes, the lilies of the field! Exactly! Isn't it ideal to preach about them—at Christmas, for instance?

Pastor Jón: Oh no, better to be silent. That is what the glacier does. That is what the lilies of the field do.

Embi: Are you sure the flowers are silent? If a sensitive enough microphone were placed beside them?

Pastor Jón: You are welcome to take the pulpit, young man. We'll have the nails out of the church door in a trice.

Embi: I can of course take the pulpit for you, since I'm supposed to be a theologian; but I don't see how that would help matters much. I wasn't sent here to be your curate, in fact, and besides, I am not ordained. I'm inquiring about parish life and the discharge of pastoral duties. And I have instructions to make an inspection of the church.

Pastor Jón: Then I shall have to fetch a crowbar. But first I suggest we have a cup of coffee and some genuine Thunderer. To tell you the truth it's a long time since I had anything to eat. Do you mind if I light my namesake, the primus?

It would have been hardly polite to decline the hospitality of a man who was so much my superior in years and dignity. Indeed, I had already successfully withstood two tidal waves of coffee that morning along with the obligatory flotsam of sweetcakes. Perhaps what settled it was hearing the pastor mention good honest rye bread, even though he gave it a name in keeping with his own scant orthodoxy. He went inside the shed and I watched him manipulate the primus: pour meths into the bowl, light it and wait until the burner heated up, close off the air in the container, and then start pumping the paraffin with all his might up through the glowing burner; and a violet flame formed; this was accompanied by the romantic sound of a waterfall; the whole procedure just as the parish clerk, Tumi Jónsen, had described for me in outline. The pastor had some water in a bucket, and coffee in a tin. When the water began to boil he sprinkled ground coffee haphazardly from the tin into the kettle. He stirred the foaming coffee with a file so that it wouldn't boil over. Then he produced a handsome loaf of black pot-bread, dug into his pocket for a clasp-knife, and cut some generous slices, never less than three centimetres thick. He kept some butter in an earthenware jar among a pile of rusty scrap-iron, and said the iron kept it cold so that it didn't melt even if the shed got hot on a summer's day. He gouged the butter out of the jar with a chisel; nor was there anything stingy about the helping. He told me to put it on with my clasp-knife, and if I didn't have one, to spread the butter with my finger, and he taught me the method: the right thumb is applied obliquely, that's to say, to form an angle of nearly thirty degrees against the bread. He apologised for the fact that his hands were too dirty to do it for me himself. Then he poured coffee into two old earthenware jars that had no doubt originally contained Danish jam of the kind that was imported early this century. These jars hold nearly half a litre. From a square tin he spooned out with a putty knife an enormous quantity of brown sugar into the coffee so that it nearly brimmed over the jars, and he stirred both our mugs with a six-inch nail. We sat down again on the bench by the shed directly facing the glacier, and started swilling down this sugary-sweet kettle-coffee and biting into these thick slices with their mountains of butter the like of which one has to go to Denmark to see. Perhaps it was margarine, by the way. Or what? I don't care; it was a marvellous feast whatever anyone says, and I couldn't help exclaiming: What matchless bread!

Pastor Jón Prímus: Old women all over the place keep me in pot-bread. It varies a bit actually, but it's never downright bad; at least I never suffer any ill-effects. And this is rather a good woman we've got today, perhaps we'll have her tomorrow as well. (Pointing to my shoes): What a beautiful pair of shoes you have, by the way. How much do shoes like these cost in the south nowadays?

I guessed at the price, and he thought it high.

Pastor Jón: But it's a pleasure to own beautiful shoes. Once I had a beautiful pair of shoes and a girl.

Embi: And now?

Pastor Jón: I have the glacier, and of course the lilies of the field: they are with me, I am with them; but above all, the glacier. No wonder it infects these excellent girls around here! In the old days when I got tired I used to look forward to falling asleep with the glacier in the evenings. I also looked forward to waking up to it in the mornings. (Here the pastor smiles lyrically and looks at me.) Now I am beginning to look forward to dying from this highly responsible office and entering the glacier.

14

*Inventory of the
Parish Church
at Glacier*

Vegetation. All around the church and right up to it the grass is tall, and all still withered. The lych-gate consists of weathered, rotting pieces of wood just visible above the old brittle grass. What the Edda says about the paths to houses that no one visits applies also to the path to the church. The derelict external condition of the church was described earlier; no need to elaborate further.

Entrance. First, the threshold. This threshold as measured by the undersigned was forty-eight centimetres above ground. Cannot see how members of the congregation can gain entry into God's House if one excepts gymnasts in the prime of life. For the reason stated, it seems that people who are lame or rheumaticky, elderly women and greybeards, would not be happy to come here. Pastor Jón says in reply that a set of steps with a few rungs must have been removed for other purposes. No one had complained about this arrangement. The steps were not missed.

Over the church door there is a kind of gable-head or rafter made of two deal boards, for ornament and protection. This gable has been in some sort of architectural relationship with the entrance door and both were once brown, but gradually they have become colourless through decay and weathering. Door-latch out of order. The lock gone. Hinges awry, mountings rusted through. Three boards form a bar across the church door, and their ends have in fact been securely nailed to the doorposts, the idea doubtless being to prevent this double door blowing open in a storm.

The pastor explains that the bishop himself had looked at these church doors some years ago and thought them good, at least not raised any objections, but not gone inside. Whereupon in the name of the Lord and the Forty Holy Knights, let's try to get this church open, says pastor Jón Prímus.

The pastor now gets busy with the claw hammer. As soon as each board is prised loose he pulls out the rusty nails and puts them in his pocket. He manages to ease the door from the doorposts even though the hinges are in poor condition. Everything creaks and groans. The inner door was painted a light colour with oak patterns, and it screeched evilly when it was opened. Dark in the church; a smell of rot and decay gushed out to meet us. The undersigned requests that the wooden shutters be torn from one or two windows, and the pastor obliges and a glimmer of daylight enters. A gust of air swept through the decaying building. The floor heaved, like a quagmire. Water has obviously got into the foundations and has rotted the floorboards. White fungus throve in the black mould-patches on the floor and ditto on the damp-stained wall panelling, which seems to have been painted blue originally.

Altar rails (Latin *gradus*). The altar rails tottered on four balusters. The kneeler is meant to provide comfort for communicants when they kneel, and at one time had been upholstered with red cloth, but it is now mouldered, torn, and mouse-eaten, with the horsehair padding showing through the cloth, and it could well be that living creatures inhabit it; but insects rather than mice.

Embi: What can have happened to the missing balusters from the altar rails?

Pastor Jón: The children made off with them when the church was unlocked.

Embi: And you have done nothing about it?

Pastor Jón: They think it sport to beat cows with a nicely turned decorated stick.

Chalice and paten. Concerning these treasures the pastor replies to the effect that thieves took away everything of that sort a long time ago. But there's a rather clumsy old brass candlestick on the altar. If you want it, says the pastor, I shall close one eye. I myself have stolen nothing here. But I accept responsibility for the removal of the church pews.

Church pews.

Embi: So you have had the pews removed, pastor Jón?

Pastor Jón: We were compelled to do that during the firewood shortage in the spring of the great snows. It was two hundred kilometres to the nearest lump of coal. All means of transport were immobilised right until May.

Embi: What did the parishioners say?

Pastor Jón: Oh, well, it was the parishioners who carried the pews away by themselves in the great snows. With my permission, in fact.

Embi: I thought people were well-to-do here?

Pastor Jón: No one, least of all the well-to-do, thinks himself too good to wade home through the snow with his church's furniture on his back. It's only the well-to-do who can afford to accept anything as a gift. I myself had nothing to put under the kettle except my furniture, and the books, and in the last resort the doors of the parsonage. Yes, it's a high office, this.

Retable, etc. The east gable wall is in poor condition. The damp has attacked the altarpiece, which is an ancient triptych; there were once three pictures, the main one in the middle. The wing-panels are on hinges and should close over the centre-piece, and this had doubtless been done for many hundreds of years whenever there was no service in the church. Damp has now got at the wood from behind and has spread to the painting, so that the pictures look as if they had been smeared with tar.

Embi: What were these pictures?

Pastor Jón: They were great pictures, Bible pictures.

Embi: Nothing special?

Pastor Jón: Oh yes, yes, indeed they were. I seem to recall the Crucifixion was the centrepiece.

Embi: What about the wing-panels?

Pastor Jón: There were some saints. To tell you the truth I never had a proper look. These were old and good pictures.

Embi: They're in pretty poor condition now.

Pastor Jón smiles: I am prepared to guarantee they have never been as good as now.

Pulpit. Sometime or other a bundle of desiccated sticks

painted in olden times had been placed on the floor against a wall; there are still some remnants of figures and lettering on them.

Embi: What is that pile of sticks, if I may ask?

Pastor Jón: That is the pulpit.

Embi: In somewhat strange condition, is it not?

Pastor Jón: Oh, I wouldn't say that. Don't all pulpits get like this? I don't suppose it makes much difference. A well-to-do farmer nearby had run out of sticks like so many others in the spring of the great snows. He was feeling rather sorry for himself, poor devil. He said everyone had been given wood except he. So I said he could have the pulpit. He had finished dismantling it and had split the boards and tied them up with string, was going to fetch them the next day. But then the thaw arrived and the roads were becoming passable and one could fetch things from town.

Chandelier (Danish, *lysekrone*). In a corner, a heap of scrap-silver, or rather of some sort of grey-gilt metal, probably silver-mixed copper, fragments of repoussé and embossed silverwork. A quantity of links and scraps of broken-off chain-hangings, along with a number of matching candlesticks with not very intelligent-looking lion-heads; furthermore, wings, heads, and feet of angels: rather late German Romanesque style (*spätbarok*). Pastor Jón volunteered the information that this was the church chandelier and called it by the Danish name, and used the word "she" about these said fragments.

Pastor Jón: She hung from the ceiling. She was too heavy for the ceiling. She fell to the floor.

Embi: And no one had time to hang her up again?

Pastor Jón: She is unfortunately in 133 pieces. But my friend the bishop is welcome to hang her up again.

Embi: And you're supposed to be so good at mending primuses, pastor Jón!

Pastor Jón: And correspondingly bad at Baroque art.

Embi: How do you know there are 133 pieces? Who has had time to dismantle this work of art so carefully? Or to count the bits?

Pastor Jón: No one is so busy that he hasn't the time to dismantle a work of art. Then scholars wake up and count the pieces. There have been untold thousands of churches in Iceland down the ages, all full of works of art. Where are these works of art now? A' b'oken, say the children.

Embi: In other words, the children have ruined everything!

Pastor Jón: As a matter of fact, others are ready to help. There is for instance the Weather; and there is the Law of Gravity; and last but not least, Time. These are tough fellows. Night and day, always at it. And at it still. No one is a match for them.

Musical instruments. The pastor says that everyone agrees that there was an organ here once. It disappeared. No one knows when. No one knows who saw it last.

Church bell. Not possible to examine the bell; the stair to the belfry was taken away during the spring of the great snows.

15

Le Cimetière Délirant, i.e., the Best Churchyard in the Land

We went out into the drunken churchyard and sat down on a tombstone under a reeling cross that was trying not to fall on its back in the withered grass. The sun shines on the glacier; it has once again moved closer. It was tantalising this morning as it was tearing off the last shreds of fog; by midday it had come quite close, and yet one wanted it to come even closer. But when it is as close as this, it is as if one suddenly sees the sweat-pores on a girl one has loved at a distance. One no longer wants to go nearer. Here's hoping it doesn't now lead to contempt! At any rate, the eye becomes dull and thought stands still.

Embi (using pocket recorder and shorthand notebook): I know it's unnecessary to make the point that this churchyard is only fair to middling, pastor Jón, and barely that.

Pastor Jón: Best churchyard in the land.

Embi: You realise, pastor Jón, that it is my duty to describe the church and churchyard for the bishop to the best of my conscience and ability as I see it.

Pastor Jón: Please yourself.

Embi: I suppose for the record I ought to set down your answers to a few questions concerning congregational life and the administration of the parish. Easier to get it from your own lips than piecing it all together from here and there. Now, the churchyard and church are so-so, as we know. But a building has gone up over there so close to the church that its corner almost collides with it, and would block the view and the sunlight in God's House had there been a window there. Who built this house?

Pastor Jón: Has it never occurred to you that the word *house* doesn't mean *house* and has nothing to do with a house?

Embi: I hope that you are nonetheless pastor Jón?

Pastor Jón: Out of the question.

At first Embi says: Well, that complicates matters; then he sighs and adds: What can we do about it?

We both gaze perplexed into the blue for a while. Finally pastor Jón says: Should we not come to an agreement like little children do when they start playing? Otherwise there could be disagreement. Shall we not say, This is to pretend to be a house? And I am to pretend to be called pastor Jón Prímus?

Embi: Thank you very much, pastor Jón. That was an excellent idea. It's going to be all right now. Might I then ask what is the man who built that house to pretend to be called?

Pastor Jón: Godman Sýngmann.

Embi: Any relation of Syngmann Rhee?

Pastor Jón: Professor and Doctor.

Embi: German?

Pastor Jón: What, Mundi Mundason? Oh no, no. A lot of

things can be said about Mundi, both good and bad, but German he has never been to the best of my knowledge.

Embi: Professor Doctor is a German title.

Pastor Jón: Perhaps such titles can be acquired somewhere, for cash down. The late pastor Jens of Setberg used never to reply to anyone who called him pastor.

Embi: Is he an Icelander, this man? And if so, who are his people and where is he from?

Pastor Jón: We were comrades, though he was almost ten years older than I and had become an engineer and inventor all over the world by the time I eventually graduated. He is descended from corner-shops and all manner of business agencies in the Vestfirðir (Westfjords) for centuries back. We owned the glacier together, each from his own side. No one in these parts doubts that the glacier is the centre of the universe. After that I received the benefice here at Glacier. He was home on leave that spring. I invited him to come and pitch his tent behind the church once I was settled in and married. When I had been installed in office here, I went back south to fetch my bride and my guest. But he was gone. I did not see him again for thirty-three years, until suddenly he was standing there in my house with a fishing rod and a gun, and said he was here to pitch his tent.

Embi: What do you wish to say about this peculiar building on the glebe here?

Pastor Jón: They can set off with that thing whenever they like and wherever they like, as far as I'm concerned. I look upon it as a tent.

Embi: Can it be set on record that this building has been erected without the pastor's permission, and that the church authorities may remove it whenever they wish?

Pastor Jón: You can set down what you like.

16

Marital Status of
Pastor J. Prímus

Embi: One further detail: there's been some talk in higher places about the marital status of pastor Jón Prímus. I'm not going to start interfering in that. But what causes a clergyman to attract unbecoming gossip arising out of his private life?

Pastor Jón: I have no private life. Let alone secrets. What are you trying to ask?

Embi: You said you had gone south to fetch your bride.

Pastor Jón: At the time I was ordained to this living thirty-five years ago, then three years short of thirty, I knew a girl. She was one of those phenomena where it's difficult to tell whether it's a mirage or an earthly being, and that has never been possible to explain except in the light of Jón Árnason's folktales.

Embi: English, Spanish, Irish?

Pastor Jón: Just from a croft down on the coast to the east. The parents of such girls send them away at confirmation age to earn their living as Cinderellas in the capital. Then suddenly it emerges that they are supernatural beings. When they are divested of their rags they are queens. They gain dominion everywhere around them wherever they are placed. They cannot help it. They transcend all other people. Men find satisfaction in kneeling before them; the lady of the house starts emptying their chamber pots for them. That was the kind of girl she was. Her name was Úa.

Embi: What's the derivation?

Pastor Jón: Someone said it was compounded from the first and last letters of Úrsúla, which means *she-bear*; or even Úranía, who is goddess of the astral world. One theologian thought it was the Greek letters alpha and omega—in reverse order. Perhaps the name came about because when men happen to look at such women they start to ooh-a, like male eiderduck.

Embi glances through his notes from the morning, written in indistinct shorthand with the pages all mixed up: Is it one of those women who are said never to have washed?

Pastor Jón: She was always clean.

Embi: Never read a book?

Pastor Jón: Knew everything.

Embi: And no one ever saw her eat?

Pastor Jón: Always satisfied. Always happy.

Embi: Did you see her sleep, pastor Jón?

Pastor Jón: No, that I did not see.

Embi: Hmm, never slept either?

Pastor Jón: Always awake.

Embi: I'll set that down.

Pastor Jón: Please yourself.

Embi: Did I understand it correctly that she had been your bride?

Pastor Jón: Yes, she was my bride.

Embi: And therefore is your wife by law?

Pastor Jón: Well, that might be putting it too strongly. The wedding night never happened. Such women are a miracle.

Embi: The alpha and omega of power-lust!

Pastor Jón: In the same way as the mother's womb.

Embi: I really cannot set that down. The bishop would think I had gone mad.

Pastor Jón: I wish you could get to know this woman some time, young man.

Embi: What for?

Pastor Jón: You would understand life.

Embi: Life? What life?

Pastor Jón: What life? Yes, that's just it! I did not understand it until my bride had vanished with my friend.

Embi: A miracle—is that the same as a sign from heaven?

Pastor Jón: As you please!

Embi: In other words, Sýngmann stole the thunder?

Pastor Jón: In actual fact she was not stolen. Sometimes we lead the devil into temptation, as the late pastor Jens used to say; and that one should not do. It can result in God taking us. And that was probably not the intention.

Embi: I am a young man and it's easy to fill me up with lies. But I hope the story you've been telling me has some truth in it.

Pastor Jón: Isn't that expecting too much of pastor Jón Prímus?

Embi: You have studied history!

Pastor Jón: Oh, that never came to very much.

Embi: One final point, which hardly concerns your office except perhaps indirectly: it's said that a coffin was taken up onto the glacier some years ago. Is there any truth in that? And if there were, would there be anything crooked about it? What's in the coffin?

Pastor Jón: I do not know. I never heard.

Embi: I'm not suggesting there was any felony involved—if there had been, the police would have been sent here instead of me long ago. But I would like to hear from your own lips if there is any truth in the rumour that someone has lodged a corpse in the glacier behind the parish pastor's back.

Pastor Jón: My parish clerk Tumi Jónsen and all those folk are historians. I am a theologian.

Embi: You have been to university, pastor Jón.

Pastor Jón: When I discovered that history is a fable, and a poor one at that, I started looking for a better fable, and found theology.

17

Philosophy at Glacier

We seem to have strayed into philosophy unintentionally, so I propose we take trivialities off the agenda. I noticed when we were drinking our coffee that you said you were an adherent of the lilies of the field, and the glacier. Are these miracles too? Or a key to a German theory of cognition? Perhaps a revelation as well?

Pastor Jón: It's a pity we don't whistle at one another, like birds. Words are misleading. I am always trying to forget words. That is why I contemplate the lilies of the field, but in particular the glacier. If one looks at the glacier for long enough, words cease to have any meaning on God's earth.

Embi: Doesn't the dazzle cause paralysis of the parasympathetic nervous system?

Pastor Jón: I once had a dog that was a stray for so long that he had forgotten his name. He didn't respond when I called him. When I barked he came to me, right enough, but he didn't know me. I am a little like that dog.

Embi: Forgive me if I don't entirely agree with the comparison you have applied to yourself, pastor Jón. You remind me rather of those blissful people in religious paintings—the ones who smile while they are being hacked to pieces. In other respects, I wouldn't dream of contradicting what you say.

Pastor Jón: Sometimes I feel it's too early to use words until the world has been created.

Embi: Hasn't the world been created, then?

Pastor Jón: I thought the Creation was still going on. Have you heard that it's been completed?

Embi: Whether the world has been created or is still in the process of being created, must we not, since we are here, whistle at one another in that strange dissonance called human speech? Or should we be silent?

Pastor Jón: You must not think I am asking the bishop's representative to be silent. I merely think that words, words, words and the Creation of the world are two different things, two incompatible things. I do not see how the Creation can be turned into words, let alone letters, hardly even a fiction. History is always entirely different to what has happened. The facts are all fled from you before you start the story. History is simply a fact on its own. And the closer you try to approach the facts through history, the deeper you sink into fiction. The greater the care with which you explain a fact, the more nonsensical a fable you fish out of chaos. The same applies to the history of the world. The difference between a novelist and a historian is this: that the former tells lies deliberately and for the fun of it;

the historian tells lies in his simplicity and imagines he is telling the truth.

Embi: I set down, then, that all history, including the history of the world, is a fable.

Pastor Jón: Everything that is subject to the laws of fable is a fable.

18

About the Creation of the World, God's Name among the Teutons, etc., at Glacier (Summary)

Now for some compression and editing for a while, to try to break up the dialogue format on the tape because that by itself has neither substantive nor formal value in a report; the conversation will now be turned into indirect speech as occasion warrants, and all digressions, repetitions, and irrelevancies will be excluded; but not, I trust, so completely that no trace remains of pastor Jón's personality.

The bishop's emissary opens this part of the interview with a neutral comment, a link with what has gone before: It's an old saying that one still has to know something, despite everything.

Pastor Jón replies: I wouldn't be surprised if one comes closer to the Creation in the fable than in the true story, when all's said and done. (No comment on my part.)

The pastor explains that "some people," as he calls them without mentioning names, consider that the Stone Age was the golden age of humanity. Those chaps knew everything they needed to know, like birds. They knew the basic principle of ball-bearings, and used this knowledge to move rocks (he probably means the sarsens of Stonehenge). But they had no alphabet and therefore they left no history behind them except their graves. For thousands of years sages have inhabited India. They had already written the Bhagavad Gita, the greatest book in the world, several centuries before Plato was born. They sit and gaze wide-eyed into the blue, but they have no history. For that reason they were unaware of it when Alexander the Great came and conquered India; they did not notice it. They learned about it from abroad two thousand years later. Emissary asks if he may set down that the principle of ball-bearings is closer to the Creation than history. Pastor Jón says that perhaps one gets closest to the creation of the world in mathematical formulae, but adds: Unfortunately, I don't know any mathematics.

Embi: Does God know trigonometry?

Pastor Jón Prímus: The creation of the world is founded on addition, I would think.

Embi: Everything supernatural is obviously over and done with long ago here at Glacier!

Pastor Jón says that these were not his words—exactly. He thinks there is one thing at least that man does not understand.

Embi: Supernatural?

Pastor Jón thinks that time is the one thing we can all agree to call supernatural. It is at least neither energy nor matter; not dimension, either; let alone function; and yet it is the beginning and end of the creation of the world.

The undersigned asks if there are any new and unexpected tidings of God here at Glacier. Pastor Jón smiles and asks if I know what the word means. When the question is referred back to the pastor himself, he relates that when he was a young man at university the authorities once made him study Old High German. Then it emerged that *god*, as we say in Germanic languages, is originally not a name for anything. It isn't even a noun. It is the past participle of a verb that means *adorare*; as time passed it became a verbal noun: *god* is that which is worshipped, *das angebetene*; "the worshipped." In one Old High German poem it is even said of God: "He is the finest of men." We Teutons, in point of fact, don't have the actual concept of God at all, don't know what it is.

Embi: I cannot see that it makes very much difference.

Pastor Jón: No, none at all. Except that God has the virtue that one can locate Him anywhere at all, in anything at all.

Embi: In a nail, for instance?

Pastor Jón, verbatim: In school debates the question was sometimes put whether God was not incapable of creating a stone so heavy that He couldn't lift it. Often I think the Almighty is like a snow bunting abandoned in all weathers. Such a bird is about the weight of a postage stamp. Yet he does not blow away when he stands in the open in a tempest. Have you ever seen the skull of a snow bunting? He wields this fragile head against the gale, with his beak to the ground, wings folded close to his sides and his tail pointing upwards; and the wind can get no hold on him, and cleaves. Even in the fiercest squalls the bird does not budge. He is becalmed. Not a single feather stirs.

Embi: How do you know that the bird is the Almighty, and not the wind?

Pastor Jón: Because the winter storm is the most powerful force in Iceland, and the snow bunting is the feeblest of all God's conceptions.

The undersigned asks if this latest proof is not a trifle circular, like the arguments about the stone that was too heavy. However that may be, I am prepared to set down that the pastor's revelation embraces *inter alia* the lilies of the field, the glacier, and the snow buntings.

Pastor Jón: Did you remember to set down, as regards the Almighty, that we are at liberty to locate it where we like and call it what we wish?

Embi: Okay.

Finally I ask pastor Jón if there is anything I ought to add. He thinks there is not much need of that, but he expands the idea a little nonetheless, albeit without commitment: Whoever worships a mountain, as countless peoples have done, then the mountain is his god; a stone if you adore a stone; a tree trunk if you believe in a tree trunk; and so on; rivers, water in a spring, water in a bowl; fish, bread, wine; a calf no less than a fairy ram; nor is the Virgin Mary in painted wood any inferior to that old widow with the big crotch, Madame Libido, or the skinless ogress Revolution, which feeds on human sacrifice.

19

Twelve Tons

The roaring twelve-ton truck is driven across the homefield, straight over the green pasture, so that the earth trembles and the calf kicks out. The monster comes to a halt among the dandelions and buttercups on the grass-grown pathway between the church and the parsonage. Out steps a broad-built man with a straddling walk (jaunty-arsed, as it used to be called) and broad-faced in the sense that the word broad-whiskered is used about a cat. His sideburns reach down as far as the lobes of his ears.

The following items of freight are unloaded:

1) Three men wearing ponchos as outer garments with an opening in the middle through which their somewhat hirsute heads protrude. This cold-weather garment is usually named after the Bronco-Indians of South America, and they wear it when they ride their special bronco-horses herding bronco-

livestock in winter; thus everything is called after bronco—horses, men, and harness. For my own convenience I shall call these fellows winter-pasture shepherds, as that was the first type of human being that came to mind when I saw them;

2) Boxes and drums made of wood, tin, and plastic; merchandise, presumably provisions;

3) Mrs. Fína Jónsen with scrubbing brush and soap.

The winter-pasture shepherds rush off into the field at once to visit the calf. One of them brings out from under his poncho a stringed instrument with a convex base, and plucks at a string to entertain the stirk; it was a somewhat weak-toned lute. They assume Buddha postures on the grass around this wretched cloven-footed animal; one takes a flower from his hair and offers it, but the stirk refuses to accept it (probably a plastic flower).

The broad-shouldered man in charge has taken Mrs. Fína Jónsen past the church and up to the front door of the bungalow; he produces a key and unlocks this mysterious house as if he lived there. Madam goes in with the scrubbing brush. Now the man in charge carries the lorry's load into the house, piece by piece. With that done he pulled a bottle from the pocket of his parka, took a drink, and pissed luxuriantly to the four winds. He happens to glance towards the parsonage; on the remains of a wall that once enclosed a vegetable garden he sees a man sitting—the undersigned emissary of the bishop. No sooner does the newcomer set eyes on this person than he walks straight over to him.

Newcomer: Hi, mate, are you a bishop, were you looking for me?

Embi: Who are you, if I may ask, sir?

Newcomer: Me? I'm just a common workingman, if you don't mind. No formality with me—I address God and my dog in the same way. So why not you as well, even though you're a bishop?

Embi: I am not a bishop.

Newcomer: Well who the hell are you, then?

Embi: Excuse me, but are you the owner of that vehicle?

Newcomer: I'm just an ordinary Icelander, if that's all right by you. Have a smoke? Have a drink? Won't have one, no. A toffee-nose, eh? I'll have you know that even though I'm just an ordinary Icelander, I've supplied whole communities and townships with sand and gravel and cement and rubble right round the bay; fetched all the materials for the quick-freezing plants in this county, and I don't mean just one or two, which the state lends you the money to build and run, then pays the losses and shoulders the bankruptcies while you yourself scram with the profits; and by these buildings Iceland stands or falls, and anyone who doesn't listen to the programme about the bankruptcies of the quick-freezing plants on the radio isn't an Icelander. And you'll have me to deal with if you won't take a drink with a chap, even though he's just an Icelander and a workingman!

Embi: Though you might be something you're ashamed of, I for my own part don't much mind about people's standing, perhaps because I have none myself. I only ask, may I have a word with you, sir?

Newcomer: How dare you be formal with an ordinary Icelander and workingman! I run a piece of industrial machinery here that is twelve tons and eighteen wheels and wears out roads at the rate of thirty-five thousand cars. Where's your car?

Embi: I've never owned a car. And this is the first time I've spoken to a man who drives a twelve-ton truck. It so happens that I was sent up here on a small mission by the church authorities. Still, it's quite obvious that you with these twelve tons are much closer to the Omnipotence than I am.

Newcomer: I've got some real Danish akvavit lovely and warm in my hip pocket. Come and sit down on a tomb! Aren't we related, by the way?

Embi: I must ask you to excuse me.

Newcomer: You're a bishop. You've got the Holy Spirit. But what God do we common Icelanders have besides Black Death booze, if it isn't warm Danish akvavit? Would you like a punch on the nose?

Embi: It makes no difference whether I'm punched on the nose or not: I simply cannot get warm akvavit down. It's like lubricating oil. It sticks in the throat. But if you're in a bad mood just now, I'd like to have your name and address for later on.

Newcomer: I'm a son of the common people.

Embi: Isn't that rather a vague address?

Newcomer: D'you think you're too good to be an Icelander?

The undersigned finally lets himself, for demagogic reasons, be talked into accepting the bottle, and pours a few drops of tepid akvavit into his palm and rubs it into his hair. This the twelve-tonner man doesn't like; he snatches the bottle from me and curses me again in no uncertain terms, but ends his comments on a resigned note with the phrase "stick to what you fancy," takes a pull from the bottle, and puts it back in his pocket.

Newcomer: My name is Jódínus Álfberg. I'm a poet. I shall now recite the Palisander Lay, written by me.

Embi: Unfortunately I don't have enough tape to record a poem.

Jódínus Álfberg: Not an Icelandic vein in your carcass! But between you and me and the gatepost, my old woman and me have got a palisander-wood kitchen just like the rest of you down south. I've got so much palisander it makes me puke. The old woman too. I've had the kitchen painted with zinc-white.

Embi: Where does all this palisander come from?

Jódínus Álfberg: I represent the Tycoon who bosses heaven and earth.

Embi: Oh? Has some new tycoon started bossing all that?

Jódínus Álfberg: My Tycoon—he's the tycoon on whose behalf I have transported three world saviours, so to speak, to this address here today to redeem the world. They're sitting over there beside the calf. They can resurrect this whole grave-yard and tell all its occupants to skedaddle home without a word. But it's me and no one else in the land who has the key to the house. I can enter this house whenever I like and swipe whatever I like. I can take a woman in here whenever I like. I get Fína to scrub here every spring and autumn at hourly rates, even though there isn't a speck of dust or dirt anywhere: every-thing paid for in California against invoice. And I have com-plete control of the scrubbing brush.

Embi: I'm gradually beginning to understand whom you're talking about all the time, although I find it a little hard to imagine what this person looks like. What I'd like to know now is, where does he get the money?

Jódínus Álfberg: Money! The Tycoon! Don't you know he's got chain stores all over the world? Don't you know it was he who invented the secret of the submarine and the parachute?

Embi: No.

Jódínus Álfberg: Don't you realise, man, that before he invented the secret, submarines couldn't come up to the sur-face? And parachutes couldn't come down to earth? Now all submarines can come up to the surface and all parachutes can come down to earth. He sells his patents to the generals in huge quantities. All military nations owe their lives to him. In return, all military establishments have to pay him annual royalties for the patents. When everyone who trades in fish and bread has gone bust, his shops will remain. Now he's patented a method of resurrecting the dead.

Embi: While I remember, since you mentioned Mrs. Fína Jónsen, I got the impression from her this morning that you would probably be the person who knew something about a certain transportation that is said to have taken place up on the glacier a few years ago. Do you know anything about it?

Jódínus Álfberg: How was the stuff packaged?

Embi: That I don't know.

Jódínus Álfberg: And the address?

Embi: That's precisely why I'm asking.

Jódínus Álfberg: My motto is strong packaging, clear addressing.

Embi: I'm asking about contents.

Jódínus Álfberg: If the packaging and addressing aren't in order, I swipe the contents. That's what all hauliers do.

Embi: It's a pity we aren't about equally drunk, to understand one another. All the same, I would like to call your attention to the fact that if you have transported a body up onto the glacier and buried it there, that is contrary to the law of the church.

Jódínus Álfberg: I'm an impoverished workingman.

Embi: Even so.

Jódínus Álfberg: Workingmen do nothing for nothing. It's only posh people who do something for nothing.

Embi: In other words, you won't talk except for money?

Jódínus Álfberg: Just let me tell you, mate, that even though I'm an uneducated ordinary Icelander, I'm just as good as any bishop. What can you pay?

Embi: Must we always be making personal comparisons? We both know how I come out of that. I haven't got a palisander kitchen. I don't own any furniture except a bookcase I nailed together for myself out of boxwood. Period.

Jódínus Álfberg: You're just a footslogging wretch, so I might just as well tell you the truth: there's a body in the casket. There you are. A body. A woman's body. A damned dead body. Go on, have a drink. Ha ha ha. Let's get on first-name terms and drink to that, and enjoy ourselves. And I'll recite the poem about the palisander.

Embi: No, for God's sake.

The undersigned wasn't nimble enough, however, to switch off the pocket recorder before the poet had managed to deliver the first stanza of the Palisander Lay:

> *Palisander wood's just right*
> *To make a kitchen look a sight;*
> *'Cause I can turn the dark to light*
> *By painting all the black zinc-white.*

20

Provisional Summary

Pastor Jón Prímus called away "on official duties" somewhere up-country this afternoon. Evening. Your emissary has spent a few hours on the preparation of his report: organised his notes, marked up the tapes, jotted down some comments and explanations. As things stand, your emissary sees little advantage to be gained from prolonging his stay here. A draft description of the church and churchyard is attached. The condition of the parsonage, preservation of church property, and so on are matters that smack of the absurd in this place. For instance, the livestock here consists of nothing but the housekeeper's calf. Food in any real sense of the term is not served in this home; in fact there is no home to speak of, either. The parish pastor makes his living as a jack-of-all-trades for the district.

To recapitulate further:

Christian observance. As far as the undersigned can see,

Christian observance is at a minimum in the district. In addition to the state of the church, there is the testimony of the parish clerk, Tumi Jónsen of Brún, albeit given with sympathy and complete loyalty towards pastor Jón; furthermore, there is the interview with the clergyman himself, both on marked spools. From this documentary evidence it will be clear that clerical duties are hardly performed at all in the parish unless ministers from outside are called in. Burials neglected. No services at Christmas, etc.

Marital status. Inquiries as instructed brought to light the following regarding pastor Jón's marital circumstances: was probably formally married, prefers to draw a veil over it, perhaps merely an empty formality, and no *consummatio.* The woman's name—various derivations from the word *Úrsúla*, pastor Jón himself says the woman was called Úa. Happened, or rather didn't happen, c. thirty-five years ago. Who performed the wedding ceremony, if it was performed, not clear. Does the undersigned have the authority to require from a parish pastor an account of a private affair that has never been a matter of controversy within the parish or outside it, but that would certainly be a case for the police if taken up officially? Bigamy can hardly enter into it. Pastor Jón's unblemished life is common talk, together with the love and respect of the parishioners; probably unique. About the woman whom pastor JP has named his "bride" in the presence of the undersigned, the only information I have is that she is from one of those ancient fishing places farther down the coast to the east that are more akin to ghost stories than reality: in these places live princesses of unusual physical characteristics that arise from the fact that they are breast-fed by wet nurses (perhaps no cows on the farm); it's said that these women walk after death, etc. Both the pastor's housekeeper and the parish clerk TJ have in my hearing called the place Neðratraðkot. The present whereabouts of the "bride" no one knows exactly. Pastor Jón says that in his youth he made friends with an engineer of Icelandic origin who before long made a fortune in other continents and called himself Professor Doctor Godman Sýngmann (Mundi Mundason, alias Guðmundur Sigmundsson, says pastor Jón). NB: Wasn't there something in the newspapers here a few years ago about an Icelander in Australia, or the Argentine, or California, who was supposed to have written six volumes about life on other planets—exobiology; privately published, I think, partly in Spanish and partly in English, places of publication rather far-off and a little peculiar, as I recall. The undersigned knows no one who has read this, but there is said to be a pamphlet available in our own language that contains a summary of this compatriot's gospel; have unfortunately not seen it. (Could this possibly be yet another example of the man from a remote island? He is a brilliant man and educated at foreign universities. He manages to make money proliferate out of the destitution in the Far East and Polynesia. After that he settles in the most frenzied and frenetic capitals the world has ever known—Paris, Buenos Aires, New York, Los Angeles. Yet the islander in him continues to dominate his soul and each year he is drawn closer and closer to the hole in Snæfellsjökull into which Professor Doctor Otto Lidenbrock plunged in pursuit of Árni Saknússemm the alchemist.)

Luxury house of choice Oriental wood. As an example of the above incongruity, which is innate in people from remote islands and consists of being unequal in size and shape to all other objects around them, I take the liberty of citing the luxury house that Prof. Dr. Godman Sýngmann has had built at an angle to the church (illustration attached). The house has been empty for three years, in the care of one Jódínus Álfberg. Regarding this building it can be stated that neither the parish pastor nor anyone else is aware of any permission having been obtained for such an edifice on glebe-land belonging to the church. Pastor Jón, however, has a vague recollection of having long ago given an old friend of his some sort of promise that he could pitch his tent here. At the time of writing, the owner of the building is said to be not far away, fishing for sea trout. The undersigned considers this house to be no concern of his or his mission. The church authorities would do better to go to law to get a decision on whether this oft-mentioned house is legal or not, and thereafter make arrangements accordingly.

Pastor Jón Prímus's doctrine. This clergyman's doctrine is on the accompanying tapes. But it isn't the whole story by any means. Regrettably the tapes are rather uncommunicative. Even though your emissary has tried to question the pastor about his innermost attitude towards the confessions of faith—to no avail. As far as I can see, however, some of the pastor's ideas possibly touch lightly upon Christian theology in places—but where are the ideas that don't? I lack the learning to analyse the mode of thinking that emerges in these tapes. I try in my questioning to take my cue from the confessions of the faith whose servant I am. Even though the undersigned considers himself a liberal in the theological profession, I would not unreservedly want to classify pastor Jón's way of thinking as liberalism, as Protestants interpret that concept. I doubt if pastor Jón is even a Únitarian as understood by the church—let alone anything more.

Towards the end of our conversation in the churchyard today I got the impression that pastor Jón thinks that all gods that men worship are equally good. In the Bhagavad Gita, which pastor Jón cites, Krishna is reported as saying, as I recall: You are free to address your prayers to any god at all; but the one who answers the prayers, I am he. Is this what pastor Jón means when he says that all gods are equally good except the god that answers the prayers, because he is nowhere? Neither of these two standpoints can be accommodated within the framework of our confession of faith. The god who speaks through Krishna's words isn't particularly pleasant, either, because he alone controls the card-game and the other gods are only dummies and he is the one who declares on their cards. At any rate this god is rather far removed from the seventy-year-old grandfather with the large beard who came to breakfast with farmer Abraham of Ur accompanied by two angels, his attendants, and settled in with him, and whom the Jews inherited and thereafter the pope and finally the Saxons. When Krishna says he is the one god who answers prayers, then this actually is just our orthodox god of the catechism, the one who says: I am the Lord thy God, thou shalt have no other gods before me. Pastor Jón says, on the other hand, Thou shalt have all other gods before the Lord thy God. What is the answer to that?

But theology apart, people here at Glacier joke about the fact that whenever pastor Jón travels from farm to farm in February he is pursued by herds of free-range horses and flocks of snow buntings and even ravens, because he keeps these creatures in food. The ethical code that moulds pastor Jón's behaviour is to be found, perhaps, in the compassion theology of the twelfth century.

Concerning a funeral on Snæfellsjökull. Whether this funeral took place behind the church's back or to some extent with its connivance, the parish pastor has nothing to say. The parish

clerk, Mr. Tumi Jónsen of Brún, ignores the question. From
the parish clerk's daughter, a middle-aged widow, was obtained
the name and address of a man who is said to have gone up
onto the glacier on behalf of Prof. Dr. Sýngmann, whom the
people at Brún call the Angler. Concerning secret deaths at Glacier at the time when this journey is supposed to have been
made—no news. Everyone got into the ground who had business there that summer according to the law as usual, though
pastor Jón often passes on to others the task of officiating at the
funerals of his parishioners, as was said before; for that matter
the people here are not perhaps suited for long funeral sermons,
although in other respects they are healthy and long-lived.

Conversation with "the Tycoon's" handyman. This afternoon
your emissary had a word with the man the widow Jósefína
Jónsen had mentioned, the poet Jódínus Álfberg. This man
appears to be the big noise in the district and drives a vehicle
that weighs twelve tons and has eighteen wheels and wears out
the roads at the rate of thirty-five thousand ordinary cars. This
man seems to have a more than usually sensitive conscience
and is mortally ashamed of three crimes that he loses no opportunity of justifying to himself and others, namely:

1) being a workingman
2) being a common man, and
3) being an Icelander.

Jódínus Álfberg himself, however, is pleased to call himself a
poet. He has composed a Palisander Lay. He claims to be the
representative of the oft-mentioned Sýngmann, whom he calls
the Tycoon. He said he was paid for keeping silent, but since he
was a wage earner he would also accept payment for talking.
When we parted he said these words to me: There is a body in

the casket; but since he got no payment, it is just as likely that he was not stating fact.

Consider that the investigation of this matter is the responsibility of other parties than the bishop's emissary. Beneath the dignity of the bishop's office to concern itself with gossip. Suggest that the Ministry of Ecclesiastical Affairs refer the case to the Ministry of Justice with appropriate report; they for their part can then call for a police investigation on their own behalf if deemed necessary.

Finally, the undersigned can see no reason for a much longer stay in the area since, as was said before, ordinary facilities for receiving visitors are not available in this parsonage. Further activity, such as sniffing around for dead people on glaciers, might be a job for the police or the Scout movement, but is an unworthy task for the spiritual authorities of the country. Furthermore, I understand that I was only scheduled to spend this one day here in the west to complete my mission. The scheduled bus leaves tomorrow morning at 1145.

21

De Pisteria

Boiled fish? Twice today your emissary thinks he has noticed a smell of fish wafting out of the "old farmhouse," that part of the house whose walls are still made of turf. This smell arouses the hunger of a visitor who has not been invited to table by his hosts all day. Can it be that the woman eats fish on the sly? Fairy fish?

Late in the evening, just when your emissary has arranged the items of his report and summarised the material (see previous chapter), Miss Hnallþóra is at the door of the guest-chamber saying, May I offer you a little cup of coffee?

It's hard to give up hope that perhaps there might be fish as well, or even just a piece of bread. The undersigned follows the woman to the spare room. Alas no fish. The table was gigantic, as if giants had been working at it. Here stood that table loaded with an abundance of all dainties as in the *Saga of the Virgin Mary*—with the exception of the one dainty: proper food. A table of such plenty provokes by its very presence the same kind of hunger-nausea in a starving man as the roots of moss-campion and seathrift doubtless did during the famines in Iceland in olden times. Add to that the smell of "chicory" (dandelion root) being boiled as a substitute for coffee out in the kitchen. Still, it's obvious how much the use of gaudy colouring on the sweet-cakes has been reduced since last night. Not only were the cakes drier and neater than before, but democratic tea-cakes were beginning to play a reasonable part, such as for instance so-called Jew-biscuits, which are rather pretty in shape, about the same thickness as oysters, and with a colourless blob of egg-white and sugar on top—it reminds one of something dried up, which there is no need to mention. Likewise there were now numerous doughnuts, which had not been seen yesterday, and so coarse, almost obscene, that it nearly shocked one's sense of decency and called to mind the doughnut-mother in China who according to the newspapers is nearly half a metre in length and proportionate in girth and stuffed three times up herself. In all, six new sorts of cakes had been added to the collection since last night. And though a detailed description of such a banquet does not directly concern this report, I cannot but emphasise the crucial change that has taken place since last night, in that a new sensation has now overthrown the war-cakes—foreign wafer-biscuits coated with melted chocolate. These are Prince Polo biscuits of the kind the undersigned was offered this morning at the parish clerk's, specially manufactured in Poland for the Icelanders. Concerning this foodstuff I refer to Tumi Jónsen the parish clerk. In itself it is no small compliment to the morals of a nation to point out that when it had become wealthy and no longer knew how rich it was, it did not copy the example of other prosperous nations by eating many kinds of steaks and pâtés on weekdays and spiced peacock on Sundays, washed down with piment and claret; instead, Prince Polo biscuits were all that the nation indulged in as a sweetener after the centuries of black pudding and whale meat.

Miss Hnallþóra: I noticed last night that the bishop wasn't much for rich cakes with spices, so I made up some plain dry-cakes and ordered from Akranes a few Prince Polo biscuits, which are so much in fashion now and thought most genteel down south.

Embi: Thank you, but I think I'll wait until the master is seated.

Miss Hnallþóra: The master? Pastor Jón? Seated where?

Embi: I hope the pastor will be so obliging as to eat with me.

Miss Hnallþóra: This is just a cup of coffee.

Embi: Thank you, but it's my custom not to drink coffee until after the meal.

Miss Hnallþóra, astonished: The meal? What is the bishop talking about?

Embi: Fish, for example.

Miss Hnallþóra: It has not been the custom here at Glacier to serve fish to the gentry. I am not going to be the first to offer a learned gentleman fish. I would be the butt of the whole county.

Embi: Why?

Miss Hnallþóra: Why? It isn't genteel.

Embi: What is genteel?

Miss Hnallþóra: Nothing less than seventeen sorts is thought genteel here.

Embi: But the pastor must eat fish every now and again, surely.

Miss Hnallþóra: The pastor has something out of his pocket wherever he happens to be. The ladies send him a loaf of rye bread occasionally; that's how they show their love for him. The drivers, too, sometimes leave something in the shed. Those who go out fishing from the glebe-lands give him a brace of fish now and then as his share of the catch, and he dries them himself on the old fish-racks out in the lava; sometimes a flounder, what's more. His dulse he dries on the rocks. And there is water in the streams. One could say that the pastor lives off the abundance of the land.

Embi: You yourself could hardly avoid tasting this, er, stuff sometimes, on the quiet.

Miss Hnallþóra: What stuff?

Embi: F-fish.

Miss Hnallþóra: It has never been thought fitting for better-class women to gorge themselves on fish in public here at Glacier.

The woman walked out, and I could see she was offended with me. This time she did not stay by me, as was the custom of the country, to ram the cakes down my throat, but left it to me to crawl out of the mess on my own. Perhaps this arrangement was a step in the right direction. Perhaps I could expect to get a simple piece of bread tomorrow or the day after. But I regretted having shocked the woman's maidenly modesty by mentioning fish. Yet now it was easier to understand why such a woman was bound to have seen a fairy ram, and likewise why Úrsalei and her kinswomen had never been seen to eat.

22

Strange Moment of Time

0415 o'clock: the sun already up and shining on the face of the pastor's sleeping guest. He swings his legs out of bed, determined to be off as soon as possible, and starts to get dressed. Consider myself in no way obliged to put up with hunger and misery here a day longer for the sake of an affair in which I think few people take much interest, least of all the parties concerned; besides, another day is unlikely to add much to yesterday as regards the prospect of salvation for souls in this part of the world. I start packing my equipment, the tapes and shorthand notes, into the duffel bag in the hope that I haven't entangled myself in anything for which I shall have to suffer later; and secondly, that I shall never be reckoned other than an impartial reporter about Christianity at Glacier.

If pastor Jón Prímus has fled the farm on my account, I send him my greetings. If Miss Hnallþóra is annoyed with me because of inhumane attitudes towards sweet-cakes, she'll just have to argue it out with herself. Consider myself beholden to no one in this place, hope that in the end the calf will get the cakes mixed in its swill. I have decided to spend the morning strolling over to the cliff-edge at the bottom of the homefield to hear what the kittiwake colony has to say, that colony where everything is multiplied a million times compared with what can be read in my report. Pastor Jón reckons that one million kittiwakes live in the sea-cliffs on this stretch of coast, which the pastor's homefield touches at one point, reaching to the edge of the cliff as was said earlier. But it seems to me just as probable that one could multiply by seven the number of these white inhabitants on the black cliffs. Most of the birds are nesting now and have started laying—and excreting. The coal-black cliffs are white. Those who love the metropolitan cities of the world would doubtless call it salvation to be allowed to sit here for the rest of their lives.

The cries of these birds are a function of their flight, for when they are sitting they are silent. Just now there reigns in their bleating that contentment which is in the nature of this strange moment of time poised between daybreak and morning. The pitch is at once gentle and full; overpowering, unerring, rhythmic. Or am I perhaps describing the audio-perceptions of the person himself who has woken up, young and healthy, while the morning is officially not yet arrived and all mankind sleeps? Every now and again there is a deathly silence. Is it an artistic silence? Or sudden news of disaster?

The egg on the very brink of the cliff is for these folk their bank account, status symbol, and confession of faith. The female goes on sitting close to her man whatever happens. It is as if her senses have been disconnected. Many of them sit motionless for hours on end and seem to be doing mental arithmetic. A few are gliding without any effort over the deeps in front of the precipice on some inscrutable errand, like snowflakes drifting in a calm. Perhaps watching out for the enemy, the fulmar. The kittiwake is *larus* and has the title of *tridactylus*, that is to say a three-fingered gull. This is like looking into another world. It is as if one gets a vision of sentient beings in the galaxies. Sometimes there is a reading from an uninspiring book or someone gives a lecture or even stumbles through a homily; here and there an old woman argues with herself in an undertone all the while. But just when they are all about to doze off in the fine weather there's always someone who starts up, though probably not necessarily the same one, and he's thought of something curious while he was sitting beside his wife and the egg; who knows, he may have felt a touch of patriotism when he was falling asleep and now bursts our with *O Iceland, Awaken!* Another one gets idealistic all of a sudden and wants to save the world without delay and takes wing with these words: Anything is better than being passive! Yet another makes himself heard above all the din just to tell a joke. A moment later there is ecstasy on the cliff again.

23

Winter-Pasture Shepherds

To pick up where we left off, when three winter-pasture shepherds had arrived here from far-off nations: the undersigned caught a glimpse of them yesterday when they got down from Jódínus Álfberg's twelve-ton truck and sat down round Hnallþóra's calf in the homefield. It is not the undersigned's job to keep an eye on bearded men. The bungalow and its people don't belong to my field of investigation.

As I stand there at the head of an inlet where the homefield ends, with a view of the cliffs to both sides, it seems to me that a shower of stones breaks over the middle of the bird colony. Stones are being hurled from the edge of the cliff west of the inlet towards the eastern face of the cliff, where the population is densest. Some of the stones miss their mark, but eventually a bird is struck and falls injured from a niche in the rock, is unable to save itself, and dies in the sea. Two or three birds that sat next to it fly up in surprise but settle again, and the accident arouses no widespread interest on the cliff. And yet a bird has just been killed there. When I look around for the cause of it I see the three men sitting on the cliff-edge.

We are loving, flower-giving apes, says the bearded one who is their spokesman and talks academic English, but out of the corner of his mouth, the American way. Beside him sits a man with a crown of flowers on his head, and my interlocutor plucks from this man's wreath a flower and throws it to me. The flower was not a genuine one. The flower-wearer's dead smile, on the other hand, was genuine, the chisel-shaped teeth regular and white as when men smile from the shadow of the mango tree in the lands where famine is routine. The white of his shining black eyes was of the same kind; his beard was a little blue; his complexion halfway between chocolate and cream-coffee. He sits there in a Buddha posture with the garland in his hair on the edge of the cliff, with his back to the ocean and facing the glacier.

The third curly-bearded one crouched on his knees with his heels under his buttocks and plucked rather feebly at some kind of a lute, and stared hard down at the instrument while he plucked, wondering what would come, then raised his eyes to the sky and watched the sound drift away, then peered muttering into the instrument as if he had lost something, before he tried again, but never quite stopped the music altogether.

It's a wonder that such dishevelled people, scantily shod and wrapped in rags, should be allowed in through Immigration! Men like this exist in Iceland only in old books and folktales, and occur in modern novels and plays only through an anachronism on the part of the authors. They herd sheep in snowstorms and wrestle with ghosts at Christmas and walk after death when the ogress has snapped their backbones. From them originates the demand in Iceland that people should be given their food without prevarication. Although violent ghosts came to an end centuries ago, it is in our natures as Icelanders to recognise these men whenever we see them, even though they are dressed in beggars' rags with lute and garland.

The bishop's emissary asks if these loving, flower-giving apes aren't winter-pasture shepherds.

First winter-pasture shepherd: I am Saknússemm the Second, the famous alchemist, the one and only person who knows the secrets of Snæfellsjökull—reincarnated in California. The one with the flowers is Epimenides. He doesn't speak. He has been asleep for fifty-seven years. He doesn't even talk in his sleep. But in his sleep he summons insects to life or kills them with his eyes. When he wakes he will speak. And Siva will stop dancing. The musician with the lute, he's the Drop; a geophysical drop.

Embi: Who has baptised you, if I may ask?

Saknússemm II: Lord Maitreya, who kindled us into human form by cosmobiological induction, has connected us with the geophysical both in the theological and historical sense. And he also baptised us. He is our lord and master.

Embi: This lord, is it a man or what?

Saknússemm II: He is bodhisattva.

Embi: Has he any quarrel with these birds?

Saknússemm II: He owns them.

Embi: Why are you annoying these birds?

Saknússemm II: They are there.

Embi: Have these birds done you any harm?

Saknússemm II: Never seen them before.

Embi: Do you know what birds these are?

Saknússemm II: Never heard of them.

Embi: Why do you want to kill these birds?

Saknússemm II: Because we love them, sir.

Embi: I don't understand.

Saknússemm II: Why do people pick flowers? Have people any quarrel with them? In our innermost selves there is something that is analogous to them. They are too good to live. We pick them and make garlands of them for ourselves because we love them.

Embi: It is certainly instructive to hear you preach, sir.

Saknússemm II: Why do people shoot animals? Because people love them, love them as themselves, love them so dearly they could eat them. The flower dwells defenceless in your innermost self.

Embi: Is this meant to be an argument for killing birds?

Saknússemm II: If someone doesn't understand, it is because he doesn't understand Siva.

Embi: Who is Siva?

Saknússemm II: Siva signifies the creation of the world and the destruction of the world. To create is to destroy. To induce life is to destroy life.

Embi: Where is that written?

Saknússemm II: The two things happen simultaneously; it is called the Dance of Siva, our god.

Embi: You sound as if you're from America. Why have you come here?

Saknússemm II: We brothers are life-inducers (NB: He actually said "bioinductors," a word the undersigned has never heard before nor seen in print. I hope this man is not a professor from Los Angeles). We have come here to bioinduct Snæfellsjökull.

Embi: By killing birds?

Saknússemm II: Killing birds is a game, like war.

Embi: Why do you Americans travel to foreign countries in order to kill birds?

Saknússemm II: War has always been the chief amusement of humankind. Other amusements are a surrogate for war. What are the Olympic Games? Bullshit.

Embi: It is monstrous to amuse oneself by killing defenceless creatures.

Saknússemm II: It has always been popular to attack the weak. A great temptation to take them on—no matter whether they are white, black, or red. A bitter disappointment when it turned out they could defend themselves; tragic; it's like pricking oneself on a rose.

Embi: Attacking the weak is considered cowardly and contemptible here in this country!

Saknússemm II: Bullshit. The weak—that's the one who dwells deepest in my innermost being. He and your flower are one. While that flower dwells inside you, you are defenceless. Destitute people know no other amusement than killing destitute people. Of all the creatures that man kills for his amusement there is only one that he kills out of hatred—other men. Man hates nothing as much as himself. That is why war is called the leprosy of the human soul.

Embi: I'm afraid that is only half the truth, my friend. At least I don't like that wording. I am a theologian. The soul has no flesh.

Saknússemm II: The soul loves lepers so dearly that it's prepared to go to the trouble of killing them all if it can kill itself at the same time. Why did the Germans tramp cheering and singing to Stalingrad? Because the Russians are the only people the Germans hope are even greater wretches than themselves. Why do we Americans travel halfway across the globe with the most complex guns in the history of the world to shoot naked

peasants in a country whose name we don't even know? It is
because we love these people as ourselves. We adore them. We
gladly pay a million dollars to be able to shoot one peasant. We
are prepared to spend the last gold coin in our treasury to be
allowed to shoot a peasant.

Embi: I would advise you not to say that out loud.

Saknússemm II: You do not understand us because you forget that in the depths of our souls we ourselves are naked peasants far beyond unknown oceans. We yearn to kill the naked
peasant within ourselves. It is our belief that he who kills a
naked peasant with a complex gun is the world's greatest.

Embi: I have always heard that in war there are two causes:
the bad and the good.

Saknússemm II: Bullshit.

Embi: Are you an anarchist, if I may ask, sir?

Saknússemm II: Football consists of one ball and one agreement. When two dogs fight they are sharing the same ideal; the
same faith. In war there is no cause except the cause of war and
that is to have a war. The leper's cause is to be a leper. Leprosy
has no cause except leprosy. Siva is dancing. Because I love you.
Bear witness, good brothers!

It was clear to me by now that I was talking to a dialectician.

The musician who bears the name of the Drop bends even
lower over his instrument and tries to make out its weak tone
against the bleating of the birds. The yogi Epimenides, the one
who has slept for fifty-seven years and bears the beautiful coun-
tenance of India's eternal famines, rises solemnly to his feet as if
he were going on an important journey. But he only turns a
half-circle. Then he sits down again on his haunches on the
edge of the cliff and smiles in his sleep over all the ocean, and
the glacier was no longer visible behind him.

24

The Red One Found, the Grey One Bolted Again

A little more than half an hour before I am due to board the long-distance bus, I catch sight of the district officer of the Langavatn people, farmer Helgi of Torfhvalastaðir, shuffling his feet on the paving in front of the house, holding a red horse by the reins. Eventually he decides to knock on the door of the parsonage, but the hammering cannot be heard in the "old house," at least it doesn't reach the leathern ears of Miss Hnallþóra. So the pastor's overnight guest goes to the door and greets the district officer of the Langavatn people.

Langvetningur: Greetings and blessings, vice-bishop! What luck for me that all the ecclesiastical authorities haven't gone with the wind! Though you're all apathetic, I'm still counting on you. I come back to the trifling matter I was mentioning old pastor Jón yesterday morning.

Embi: I congratulate you on finding the red one.

Langvetningur: Well, that's quite a story, I can tell you. When I woke up this morning down by the coast where I spent the night with the two horses, believe it or not the grey one had bolted again! Horses always head for the places where they suffer the most, up to the remote valleys or out on the headlands where there isn't enough to fill even a bunting's beak. Now I'm off to look for my grey one again, because they're both promised for a glacier trip tomorrow morning. That's the way the world goes. But thank goodness, at least I've met the same-as-a-bishop. And now I say, as the Bible puts it, I won't let you go until you bless me.

Embi: I'm just leaving for the south.

Langvetningur: It's terrible never to get peace and quiet to talk to you people from the south, and me with such heaps of things to argue with you; all in a brotherly way, of course.

Embi: Do come into my room, I'm just finishing my packing. There's not much in the way of chairs here, but you could try sitting on the edge of my bed. But I'm afraid there's little to be gained from a discussion with someone who has no special revelation, hardly even a proper creed. I'm not even any use at helping people find a stray.

Langvetningur: As you know, the Master has arrived in the district.

Embi: What master?

Langvetningur: The great Master.

Embi: Oh. Really.

Langvetningur: The last time the Master was here he got two reliable men, or let's hope they're that, anyway, to take a small box up onto the glacier. A casket. One of these men was me with my horses, the other was Jódínus.

Embi: I know what was in the casket. I should like to know

when the Ministry of Ecclesiastical Affairs gave permission for this transportation.

Langvetningur: Perhaps no one remembered to think of that.

Embi: Was this person killed, or what?

Langvetningur: That was none of my concern. I was never allowed to look into the box. But isn't that beside the point? The main point, it seems to me, is that the Master is back now, along with his submasters, three bioinductors—high reincarnations, I hope I can say—to carry out the work. The idea is that this body is to be life-induced. We need a church for the task. But pastor Jón refuses to open the church.

Embi: He opened it yesterday.

Langvetningur: He has nailed it up once more. I see no alternative but to apply to the bishop.

Embi: You're not going to land me with that lot, as the man said who refused to harbour Grettir the Outlaw. And besides I have no authority to lend this church to anyone. Least of all for such a purpose. Christianity has had its resurrection once and for all. And what's more, so far as I can see, what is to be performed here is some kind of mechanised resurrection, engineering. Churches are not for that. If I send the Bishop of Iceland a telegram, or ask him for something like that over the telephone, he would think I had taken leave of my senses.

Langvetningur: Has the bishop then not read Dr. Guðmundur Sigmundsson's books?

Embi: I haven't the faintest idea.

Langvetningur: Many would say that this church would be no worse off for being used for an experiment that without exaggeration affects future life on the earth. If it were possible to make a resurrection of life happen in a church like this, I'd call that pretty good.

Embi: This isn't much of a church.

Langvetningur: I can guarantee that the bishop has only to say the word and the Master will have a church built here worthy of being called the Glacier Cathedral and being in communion with the galaxies.

Embi: What kind of communion do you yourself have, actually?

Langvetningur: I have the same communion with the Master that the moon has with the sun.

Embi: Where did you dig up this master?

Langvetningur: When Guðmundur Sigmundsson came here to Snæfellsnes after more than thirty years' absence abroad, I was hired to ride with him on his fishing trips, show him the rivers, point out the pools and broken water, carry his baggage.

Embi: The picture I've got of this man in the course of one day is now suspiciously like the one of an elephant that four blind men conjured up for themselves not long ago, in India I think.

Langvetningur: I also thought this was just an ordinary angler and wholesaler chap until he produced his booklet, which was still in manuscript then—and then I saw what was what. In fact, an untrained country teacher of the old school was the one who helped to elucidate it; because the Master had become unaccustomed to composition in his native tongue after all these years. I was also the one who took the booklet to Reykjavík that autumn and had it published and paid the printing costs in full. I was the one who was to sell the booklet and keep the proceeds for my trouble. Unfortunately no one wanted to buy it. As it says in the booklet, in Iceland protomory and heteromory and dysexelixis prevail. No one understands bioradiophony or astrotelekinesis. And diexelixis isn't popular with the

government. I am the man who alone was chosen to understand this booklet and thereby become redeemed and reborn.

Embi: What about the poet Jódínus Álfberg?

Langvetningur: Jódínus built the house and shifted the palisander. But few would try to drive a reliquary onto Snæfellsjökull in a twelve-ton truck. For that kind of job you need the
small man with a horse. But on the other hand I guarantee, even
though I'm only a district officer in a derelict area, that the
bishop will get whatever rent he cares to name for the church.

Embi: We take the subject off the agenda. Better go and look
for the horses.

This district officer's sunshine smile is more akin to high
summer than the uncertain season between hay and grass. The
undersigned feels that someone who is looking for horses
should not let opportunities go by for himself and for others.
But he continues to expatiate.

Langvetningur: The history of mankind could well take a
new course here at Glacier on and after tomorrow.

Embi: Provided the horses are found.

Langvetningur: I'm confident that you as a young Christian
and a bishop will think twice before you exclude such an event
from the church; because despite everything, it is a holy place.

Embi, now a little snappish at continually being called a
bishop: My dear right honourable sheriff, schoolteacher, free-
holder, and turf-whale out there in Langavatnsdalur! If the faith
by which you are redeemed preaches a different resurrection
than the New Testament does, why don't you bury your whale
in the peat-bogs at Torfhvalastaðir and make it rise again there?

Langvetningur: The Master makes particular demands on
behalf of life itself, and I expect these are not entirely unknown
to the Ministry of Ecclesiastical Affairs.

Embi: What demands are they?

Langvetningur: In Guðmundur Sigmundsson's booklet, emphasis is laid on the sacred right of earthly life to a share in the power of the heavens.

Embi: I seem to recall that these are the demands that agriculture makes of the State.

Langvetningur: My master is called Lord Maitreya by his loving disciples and henchmen.

Embi: Then I think it more likely that the case has been referred to the Ministry of Foreign Affairs. By the way, it would be enlightening to hear why these broncos don't stay at home around the equator, or at least in the tropical belt, where superstitious nonsense doesn't freeze solid.

Langvetningur: People with second sight have known for a long time that some places are more susceptible to spiritual presences than others. From the locales where the All-mind has made His abode, the human intelligence has access to the Supercommunion if it can get away at all, and if it really tries. Iceland is one of the spheres for this special presence; people knew this even in the Middle Ages while hell was still in Iceland. There are special spots here where the All-thought is manifest in the elements themselves, places where fire has become earth, earth become water, water become air, and air become spirit.

Embi: I thought it was the other way round.

The Langvetningur is of the old Teachers' College and learned algebra from the Danish book by Pedersen: The order of the factors is immaterial. The main point is that here at Glacier the divine oxen of immortality will be harnessed to the plough of the soul: we are in Supercommunion, and the origins of life are in our power.

Embi: I have missed my bus because of you and am now

stranded here. But we shall come to an agreement nonetheless. I shall wait until you return from the glacier with the casket tomorrow. You will open it. And if the contents relate to theology I shall see to it that they receive ecclesiastical treatment. And now off you go and look for the hacks.

Langvetningur: I take this as a promise on the bishop's part, and bless you for making it and may God reward you and I hope I may always count on you.

Farmer Helgi of Torfhvalastaðir kisses the undersigned farewell and sets off on the red one in search of the grey. I gaze enviously after this disputatious, but in no way tedious, man who had lost his horses, to be sure, but instead had caught hold of a considerably larger horse than most men. It is to be hoped that such a man doesn't land on one of those stars in the galaxies that are 100,000 times larger than the earth and consequently 100,000 times harder to keep horses together on, not to mention find them again if they bolt.

And now there is probably nothing for it but to go and have coffee and cakes with Miss Hnallþóra.

25

Banquet of
Dried Halibut

Pastor Jón Prímus has a word with the overnight guest that evening as he sits on the edge of his bed, still glancing through his notes:

Some southerners gave me dried halibut; would you like some of that? says the parish pastor.

Strange to say "that" about dried halibut. Certainly, Icelandic doesn't have a partitive article like French, but it would have been politer and better Icelandic to have said for example: I was given fish; may I offer you some of it?

Pastor Jón Prímus: It costs £10 a kilo, they were saying—the most expensive food in the world apart from mammoth meat from the tundras.

He took me into the spare room, which resounded with emptiness since the drawers from the furniture had been used as firewood during the spring of the great snows. Then he handed me a strip of this fine white dried fish.

Embi: I feel one could well have used a stronger word than "that" about a delicacy that costs £10 a kilo.

We chewed the dried halibut lustily.

Pastor Jón: I hope there's room for quality fish like this in the report.

Embi: It's an open question whether the reporter's diet has any place in a report. Luke recorded the Acts of the Apostles, but it doesn't say what he had to eat the while.

Pastor Jón: More's the pity.

We sat on backless wooden benches on either side of the deal table on which Miss Hnallþóra would spread a cloth when she served coffee and cakes. Luckily it isn't the custom to eat dried fish off a tablecloth; dried fish lies to the north of cutlery in space and belongs to the Stone Age, or at least the Middle Ages, in time. Nor could Miss Hnallþóra restrain herself when she came into the room and saw these goings-on.

Miss Hnallþóra: May God in Heaven help and forgive the parish pastor for offering a decent man fish, and him from the south, yes the same as a bishop! And now the doctor-professor is here as well, perhaps he too is to be made to gnaw at some rock-hard dried fish! This is the absolute limit! If he bangs on the door I'm not even going to answer it; wouldn't dream of it unless I had at least thirty-five sorts. And may I add that there's a stray ewe that has started guzzling the dandelions and buttercups out on the paving; she has lost her lamb, and the professor has started pacing up and down the homefield and frightening my calf, in addition to all the Danish saviours of mankind who are here already.

Pastor Jón: There have mercifully always been sheep present whenever mankind was saved, Hnallþóra dear.

Miss Hnallþóra: Speaking for myself, if professors and doctors are going to come here on top of bishops and saviours, and the wretch of a calf dies, then I'll lock up the farmhouse and no one will get anything from me alive or dead—so now you know, pastor Jón!

26

Intergalactic Communication

Prof. Dr. Godman Sýngmann, originally Guðmundur Sigmundsson, is descended, as already stated, from merchants and commission agents or sheriffs from the trading posts farther west. He is a big, thickset old man, not too fat but heavy in the shoulders and beginning to stoop; he would probably be a full six feet tall if he were stretched. He is splay-footed, and carries his head sunk into his neck like some seabirds, the guillemot, for example, or more particularly the penguin. There is no sign of his having knees when he walks. He has an enormous face. His eyes have the moist sheen of a snake's. For an elderly man, his hair is wavy and vital, chestnut in colour and with a life of its own like Saint Olaf's beard after his death; a grey toothbrush moustache. The lower lip sags in a loop to one side; in dogs this is called baring the teeth; perhaps the professor once had a protruding tusk there that was extracted, leaving a kind of sag in the lip; perhaps the professor has also clenched his teeth too hard at one time or another. The pastor's empty room is filled by this man alone, yet he did not move much, at least never more than necessary; even his hand movements were measured, perhaps long training in self-control, or just a sign of old age. He also tended to speak in rather short sentences. A hint of a grin accompanied his words, as if the speaker expected that the listener wouldn't take them too seriously. He screwed up his eyes and looked sidelong at the person he was talking to, like an experimental scientist keeping an eye on the indicator on some sort of dial while he is making up his concoctions. Dr. Sýngmann is wearing a long and bulky windcheater jacket, and has a faded, worn old hat, badly shrunk and much too small, festooned with flies, spoons, and colourful tin minnows.

Hello, John—with these words Dr. Sýngmann makes his greeting; shaping his mouth like any elderly American, and a little hoarse.

Pastor Jón Prímus: Mundi? So you're here! Well, well. Hnallþóra thought as much. And as splay-footed as ever.

Dr. Sýngmann: And you pigeon-toed!

Pastor Jón: Yes, always stubbing my toes on my heels. The late pastor Jens of Setberg used to say that pigeon-toed people eventually turned in on themselves, and splay-footed people turned out from themselves. May I offer you a strip of dried halibut to keep a young man and myself company?

Dr. Sýngmann: No, John.

Pastor Jón: It costs £10 a kilo.

Dr. Sýngmann (in English): Skip it, John.

Pastor Jón: It's no use talking English to me.

Dr. Sýngmann: By the way, who is this good-looking young man?

Pastor Jón: He is the bishop's emissary.

The Doctor absently gives the undersigned his hand and says: Launch out into the deep, young man.

Embi: Thank you.

Pastor Jón: Have a seat, Mundi dear.

Dr. Sýngmann was holding a stick of the kind that upper-class Englishmen carry when they go horse racing; these contraptions are called shooting sticks. They can be converted into a chair out-of-doors. The stick's grip consists of two handles that can be opened out to either side to form a seat; other devices serve to stabilise it at the other end. These are what people sit on at horse races. Instead of accepting a seat on pastor Jón's wooden benches, Dr. Sýngmann manipulates his stick and sits on it. Pastor Jón Prímus becomes enamoured of this stick at once; he gets up and examines it high and low, and says he simply must get a stick like it for himself; he asks what it costs, but Dr. Sýngmann has forgotten. When the parish pastor has studied this shooting stick minutely and noted carefully how the Doctor adjusts it and sits down on it, he says: Well, old friend, where have you come from?

Dr. Sýngmann: From Ojai.

Pastor Jón: Good farming there?

Dr. Sýngmann: Yes and no.

Pastor Jón: And what are you up to yourself?

Dr. Sýngmann: I've had a house there for a few years.

Pastor Jón: What attracted you there?

Dr. Sýngmann: The light of the world.

Pastor Jón: Spin us more yarns, old chap.

Dr. Sýngmann: *Nada*, John, *nada*.

Dr. Sýngmann moved his shooting stick over to the window because that pest of a ewe was bleating outside: Nice to hear sheep bleating. We don't have many sheep in Ojai.

The undersigned isn't sufficiently knowledgeable in languages always to be able to identify a foreign accent, for instance in such a complex man as this. Often he emits a distinct American sound. Sometimes, on the other hand, there occurs a guttural *r* that could originally be an Icelandic speech defect whose roots go back to Danish summer traders, called a burr. Then suddenly there would come a Greek *chi*-sound as in the word *loch*. In Spanish this sound is denoted by a *j* in the place-name the Doctor had mentioned: Ojai.

Pastor Jón Prímus: Where is Úa?

The Doctor was a little taken aback; he turned round in his seat and looked searchingly at the parish pastor. Úa? he says, as if he had no idea what's what. She's been dead for a long time. Didn't I tell you that at the time? She sent me a telegram and said she was dead. Let's hope she's not hiding somewhere in Paris, or Switzerland.

Pastor Jón: I seem to recall, the last time you were here, you said you were going to perform a miracle on her.

Dr. Sýngmann: Did I say that?

Pastor Jón: How did it turn out?

Dr. Sýngmann: I changed her into a fish.

Pastor Jón: The devil you did! How did you manage that?

Dr. Sýngmann: *Nous sommes en route pour l'épagogique et l'astrobiologie.*

Pastor Jón: I don't speak French.

Dr. Sýngmann: I cultivate epagogics and astrobiology.

Pastor Jón: Is that so!

Dr. Sýngmann: We induce life. We induct life from one body to another: biotelekinesis. Likewise between planets, astrobioradiophony. I travel with determinants from three corners of the globe and am myself the representative of the fourth. We have been making experiments on fish. We are going to induct men into fish and fish into men. We have made such progress that we have not only raised insects from the dead but also week-old fish fry, and even minnows. In America we have a collection of individual creatures, both insects and lower vertebrates, that we have resurrected. We hope that with special methods we shall manage to preserve life for up to as much as three thousand years. Perhaps we shall one day reawaken the mummies in Egypt. This is all based on cosmobiological foundations. We have achieved intergalactic communication.

Pastor Jón: I think I'd better have some more dried halibut. (To the undersigned.) Do help yourself to more dried halibut, young man, before it resurrects. You're a great one for the tall stories, Mundi! Do carry on.

Dr. Sýngmann pulls out a leather case containing long corona cigars: Wouldn't you like a Henry Clay, John?

Pastor Jón: I'll stick to the fish. What's dried halibut in Greek, again? Well, well, old friend! But if Úa has now become a fish, and at the same time is hanging about in Paris and Switzerland, how is it possible to reassemble her?

Dr. Sýngmann: One can be one's own ghost and roam about in various places, sometimes many places simultaneously. Perhaps I didn't approach it quite correctly. A ghost is always the result of botched work; a ghost means an unsuccessful resurrection, a shadow of an image that has perhaps once been alive, a kind of abortion in the universe.

Pastor Jón: Ah yes, the universe, my children, as the late pastor

Jens used to say—that's saying something. You should offer this young theologian something good to smoke.

Mercifully no attention was paid to the undersigned in this respect; indeed, I would have been in poor shape had I started puffing at a large-size Henry Clay. In company that was so far above me, I enjoyed the privilege of being allowed to dissolve and coalesce with the elements of the air as soon as I had been greeted with a suitably meaningless compliment. I sat slightly behind the visitor, and the silent recorder ran smoothly between the changes of spools from my parka pocket. Unfortunately, for a long time there is a piercing bleat at thirty-second intervals—it's the ewe looking for her lamb outside on the paving.

Pastor Jón: Well, old chap, as always you have no small undertakings ahead of you, I should say. The resurrection of a fish, is that it?

Dr. Sýngmann: Yessir, the resurrection of the fish. It was three years ago. I happened to be here at the Bláfeldará when the telegram came saying that Úa was dead. Naturally I went on fishing. A few minutes later I had on my hook the largest salmon that has ever taken my fly in any river anywhere in the world. It took so zestfully that it snapped my rod and swam off with the stump. That evening we found the fish far down the river, where the gut had snagged round a jutting stone. It was a hen-fish. She weighed 40 pounds. I have had this fish preserved. I realise at once that this was a special fish that had a special mission. And now I have come here with my three determinants.

Pastor Jón: Is it true that these men are saviours of mankind? Or merely apostles?

Dr. Sýngmann: That would be a misnomer. I consider them to be scientists. I recruit laboratory workers, not hangers-on.

We have been investigating the law of determinants, and for that we have a laboratory in California. We draw upon the experience of at least three major religions, and furthermore, all known methods of scientific verification.

Pastor Jón: A great enterprise, my dear Mundi, a great enterprise.

Dr. Sýngmann: Could become that. Not least at Glacier. This place is unique on earth.

Pastor Jón: Yes, we here at Glacier have Snæfellsjökull. That's a fact.

Dr. Sýngmann: Iceland could set the pace in this field.

Pastor Jón: Yes, it has a very beneficial effect on people to sit here for example, just north of the homefield hillock where I have my shed and contemplate the glacier in good weather.

Dr. Sýngmann: People with second sight all over the world know this spot, have always known it. Here in the glacier is one of the most remarkable natural power stations in this solar system, one of the All-thought's induction centres. With the law of determinants one can harness this power.

Pastor Jón: Forgive me, Mundi, but what are you talking about?

Dr. Sýngmann: I am talking about the only quality that was worth creating the world for, the only power that is worth controlling.

Pastor Jón: Úa?

Dr. Sýngmann in a tired, gravelly bass: I hear you mention once more that name which is no name. I know you blame me; I blame myself. Úa was simply Úa. There was nothing I could do about it. I know you have never recovered from it, John. Neither have I.

Pastor Jón: That word could mean everything and nothing,

and when it ceased to sound, it was as if all other words had lost their meaning. But it did not matter. It gradually came back.

Dr. Sýngmann: Gradually came back? What did?

Pastor Jón: Some years ago, a horse was swept over the falls to Goðafoss. He was washed ashore, alive, onto the rocks below. The beast stood there motionless, hanging his head, for more than twenty-four hours below this awful cascade of water that had swept him down. Perhaps he was trying to remember what life was called. Or he was wondering why the world had been created. He showed no signs of ever wanting to graze again. In the end, however, he heaved himself onto the river-bank and started to nibble.

Dr. Sýngmann: Only one thing matters, John: do you accept it?

Pastor Jón: The flower of the field is with me, as the psalmist said. It isn't mine, to be sure, but it lives here; during the winter it lives in my mind until it resurrects again.

Dr. Sýngmann: I don't accept it, John! There are limits to the Creator's importunacy. I refuse to carry this universe on my back any longer, as if it were my fault that it exists.

Pastor Jón: Quite so. On the other hand, I am like that horse that was dumbfounded for twenty-four hours. For a long time I thought I could never endure having survived. Then I went back to the pasture.

Dr. Sýngmann: You are in actual fact a Mohammedan, John.

Pastor Jón: Primuses are repaired here.

Dr. Sýngmann, impatient and a little irritable: Yes, but it's out of the question! I don't accept it.

Pastor Jón: I begin to look forward to the spring during the last months of winter as soon as the first kittiwake comes flying in over the land. In summer there grows this little flower that dies. In the autumn I begin to look forward to winter, when everything falls silent except the surf, and rusted locks, useless pots, and broken knives pile up around this jack-of-all-trades. Perhaps one will be allowed to die by candlelight at Christmas while the earth sails into the darkness of the universe where God lives and all the Christmas elves.

Dr. Sýngmann: Haven't I told you over and over again, John, that I don't accept it! In this centre here on the glacier we shall produce scientific interstellar bioinduction. We shall here and now establish communion with far-off planets where life is so advanced it cannot die; do you hear what I'm saying, John! We shall not stop before the aim is achieved, with the help of the law of determinants, of inducting life here that cannot die but can only grow stronger and more beautiful.

Pastor Jón: Don't frighten me, my dear chap.

Dr. Sýngmann: We live here on the edge of space. An attempt is being made to live here. The experiment has got no further than that, as of now. Perhaps the experiment will fail utterly. We live in a world where demons prevail; murder weapons are what they live for, murder is what they believe in, but they lie about everything else. And when I say the world is governed by nothing but demons, who will continue to be demons until they have destroyed the world, I am not using profanities; on the contrary, *demon* is a scientific term, a formula covering a specific chemical composition without connotations from politics, religion, or moral philosophy.

Pastor Jón: Do you think the Creator has completely abandoned us, Mundi?

Dr. Sýngmann: I have written a revelation in six volumes. It's all in there. In my book on bioastrochemistry it is explained chemically what demons are and why they have multiplied so excessively upon earth. There is no means of destroying this lethal substance except with the help of higher sentient beings on more developed stars. In another book I have explained the law of determinants and shown how intergalactic communication depends upon knowledge of cosmobiology and biodynamics. The object is to eliminate time and distance. I have traced the fundamental elements of epagogics and epigenetics and explained how not only protomory but above all heteromory is the condition of mankind at present, and its course a fatal course: dysexelixis contra diexelixis. Namely, demons preparing to destroy all life on earth; and they will succeed in that unless they are forestalled from places in space where life has reached a higher plane.

Pastor Jón Prímus: It's terrible how poor my Greek has become, Mundi. One thing I'd like to know, though—how does my friend Helgi of Torfhvalastaðir manage to grasp all this? I would never venture upon a book by you, Mundi.

Dr. Sýngmann: My books are not yet read on earth. I have never met anyone who has read a single word of mine except Helgi of Torfhvalastaðir. Here among us on the lowest rung of the world of life, no attention is paid to books unless they are written by chemically analysed demons, or at least for them. Poets and philosophers are respected in proportion to the contempt and disgust they feel for the creation of life. Give us this day our daily war is the prayer of those who govern countries. Kill, kill, said the outlaw Skuggasveinn. *Das Leben ist Etwas das besser nicht waere*, says another obscurant, one of Germany's messiahs; and then up pipes Ketill Screech, his lackey, not wanting to be outdone: *Der Mensch ist Etwas das überwunden werden muss!* It is according to this formula that the atomic bomb was made. I ask you, John, is there any reason for accepting this?

Pastor Jón: Well, you are always on the river, Mundi, doing your best to kill fish.

Dr. Sýngmann: That's precisely why, and because all my life I have worked at improving murder weapons, and because I know from experience that murder weapons are the only things that are taken notice of here on earth—that's precisely why, John.

Pastor Jón: I'm sorry if the insignificant pastor Jón Prímus doesn't understand a word of what you're saying: these higher sentient beings in the other galaxy, the ones that are to give us eternal life—are they closer to us or farther from us than God?

Dr. Sýngmann: God—isn't he a Jew?

Pastor Jón: Oh, is that what He is? I had almost forgotten. But if that is so—and even if it were so—does that change anything?

Dr. Sýngmann: No, it changes precisely nothing. On the other hand we don't need a Jew—and even less do we need those who have stolen God from the Jews, such as the pope and Mohammed.

Pastor Jón: I didn't know you were against the Jews, Mundi.

Dr. Sýngmann: God is the god of the Jews, say I! That's why you ought to leave Him alone, John. What you have stolen can never be yours. The Jews could take these god-thieves to court and have them sentenced to prison in accordance with the Berne Convention, which prescribes heavy penalties for the theft of patents and ideas. Not to mention scandals like the one when the Christians without ceremony stole from the Jews their national literature and added to it a piece of Greek overtime-work they call the New Testament, which is mostly a distortion of the Old Testament, and, what's more, an anti-Semitic book. My motto is, leave the Jews alone. Those who deck themselves out in stolen gods are not viable.

Pastor Jón: How nice that you should come up with the word "viable," which our motorists have now started using about a new type of antifreeze. Tell me something, Mundi, are we viable, you and I? Is the world we live in viable and genuine?

Dr. Sýngmann: At least I don't ask the Jews about it; let alone the Mufti of Constantinople or the Vatican or the Patriarch of Antioch. —And at that point the Doctor notices that his cigar has gone out and he starts hunting for matches and is a little clumsy with his hands as if they are numb, and then he says: But someone must have made it all. Don't you think so, John?

Pastor Jón: Thou shalt love the Lord thy God with all thy heart and so on, said the late pastor Jens.

Dr. Sýngmann: Listen, John, how is it possible to love God? And what reason is there for doing so? To love, is that not the prelude to sleeping together, something connected with the genitals, at its best a marital tragedy among apes? It would be ridiculous. People are fond of their children, all right, but if someone said he was fond of God, wouldn't that be blasphemy?

Pastor Jón once again utters that strange word "it" and says: I accept it.

Dr. Sýngmann: What do you mean when you say you accept God? Did you consent to His creating the world? Do you think the world as good as all that, or something? This world! Or are you all that pleased with yourself?

Pastor Jón: Have you noticed that the ewe that was bleating outside the window is now quiet? She has found her lamb. And I believe that the calf here in the homefield will pull through.

Dr. Sýngmann: I know as well as you do, John, that animals are perfect within their limits and that man is the lowest rung in the reverse-evolution of earthly life: one need only compare the pictures of an emperor and a dog to see that, or a farmer and the horse he rides. But I for my part refuse to accept it.

Pastor Jón Prímus: To refuse to accept it—what is meant by that? Suicide or something?

Dr. Sýngmann: At this moment, when the alignment with a higher humanity is at hand, a chapter is at last beginning that can be taken seriously in the history of the earth. Epagogics provide the arguments to prove to the Creator that life is an entirely meaningless gimmick unless it is eternal.

Pastor Jón: Who is to bell the cat?

Dr. Sýngmann: As regards epagogics, it is pleading a completely logical case. In six volumes I have proved my thesis with incontrovertible arguments; even juridically. But obviously it isn't enough to use cold reasoning. I take the liberty of appealing to this gifted Maker's honour. I ask Him—how could it ever occur to you to hand over the earth to demons? The only ideal over which demons can unite is to have a war. Why did you permit the demons of the earth to profess their love to you in services and prayers as if you were their God? Will you let honest men call you demiurge, you, the Creator of the world? Whose defeat is it, now that the demons of the earth have acquired a machine to wipe out all life? Whose defeat is it if you let life on earth die on your hands? Can the Maker of the heavens stoop so low as to let German philosophers give Him orders what to do? And finally—I am a creature you have created. And that's why I am here, just like you. Who has given you the right to wipe me out? Is justice ridiculous in your eyes? Cards on the table! (He mumbles to himself.) You are at least under an obligation to resurrect me!

The tape ran out at this point, so I did not catch the last

arguments about the necessity of juridical quibbles to bring the Creator to his senses, nor did I catch a complete account of the wisdom of Schopenhauer and Nietzsche. I changed spools as carefully as I could, trusting that these two oldsters were so advanced in years that they had a buzzing in the ears and would not notice my fidgeting.

When the spool turns again and the tape is running, it sounds as if pastor Jón Prímus has begun to challenge epagogics with arguments that are characteristic of him: he makes no distinction between theory and fable, except that fable is for children and theories mainly serve the purpose of convincing God of some absurdity or other, or else are used as an excuse and a stalking horse for shooting.

He goes on talking.

Pastor Jón Prímus: Oh, it's all the same old hash in the same old dish. Except that in our time, philosophers and preachers have started calling themselves ideologists; theories and religions, and especially fairy tales for children, are called ideologies in every second sentence. I have only one theory, Mundi.

Dr. Sýngmann: Well, that's something! Perhaps it will save the world one day.

Pastor Jón: It is at least no worse than other theories.

Dr. Sýngmann: Let's have it, John!

Pastor Jón: I have the theory that water is good.

Dr. Sýngmann: For colds, or what?

Pastor Jón: Unqualified. One doesn't even have to go by my theory unless one is thirsty.

Dr. Sýngmann: That's poesy, John, obsolete long ago; it even says in Goethe, *grau ist alle Theorie.*

There is silence on the tape now. Later one can make out that talking has started again, low and slow; it is pastor Jón. I was hoping he would refer again to the Psalm of David about a flower, which is so good. Such quiet talk with long silences in between reminds you of trout-rings here and there in still water towards evening. But it wasn't the Psalms of David.

Pastor Jón Prímus: Do you remember when Úa shook her curls? Do you remember when she looked at us and laughed? Did she not accept the Creation? Did she reject anything? Did she contradict anything? It was a victory for the Creator, once and for all. Everything that was workaday and ordinary, everything that had limitations, ceased to exist when she came: the world perfect, and nothing mattered anymore. What does Úa mean when she sends people telegrams saying she is dead?

Dr. Godman Sýngmann has risen to his feet and has folded the seat of his shooting stick. He has started looking out of the window. The ewe lies on the paving and is chewing the cud, and the lamb lies close against her and chews the cud as well, its jaws racing. He answers pastor Jón Prímus with his back turned to him, gazing out of the window: Well, she was your wife.

27

Dandelion and Honeybee

Pastor Jón Prímus: It's perhaps too much to say that she was my wife, Mundi. Who owns a woman like Úa? Who owns the flower of the field?

Dr. Godman Sýngmann stood in the light from the window looking at the sheep, almost darkening the room with those broad shoulders in that enormous wind-cheater: It's said that the man who first compared a woman to a flower must have been a genius. The next one who parroted it was undoubtedly an ass. What are we to call the man who utters it a third time?

A rascal, replied pastor Jón Prímus, and shall undertake to be all three at once. But I hope it does not change the psalmist's words in any way. Has it never occurred to you to think kindly of God for having created the lilies of the field?

Dr. Sýngmann: Flowers? No. I am God-fearing in the fullest sense of the word. I have always been afraid of God. I have been so afraid of Him that no saint in the Middle Ages was ever more afraid of the devil. Terrible is the God who created a woman like Úa. When she had been in charge for three years of a brothel I owned in South America, I sent her to a convent. Next time I met her she had become the mother of many children in North America, separated from the men and the children dead.

Pastor Jón Prímus: Mundi, you who are so good at reading and writing books, there's one story you ought to read; I've always thought it such a good one. It is the story of the dandelion and the honeybee. May I tell it to you?

Dr. Godman Sýngmann turned round and stared at his old friend the parish pastor in amazement with those moist eyes of his with their worn red rims, at once accusing and beseeching, sorrowful and honest, humble and fierce, like the eyes of a bloodhound, that dog which bears such a dreadful name yet is nonetheless the most harmless of dogs.

Pastor Jón Prímus: There was once a dandelion and a honeybee. . . .

Dr. Sýngmann: If you are going to tell me the story of the dandelion and the honeybee, John, I shall hit you. Lyrical poetry is the most disgusting drivel on earth, not excepting theology. I'm going to bed.

Pastor Jón Prímus: When a dandelion calls to a bee with its scent to give it honey, and the bee goes off with the pollen from the flower and sows it somewhere far away—that I call a Super-communion. It would be remarkable if a more super communion could be established, even though intergalactic communications were put in order.

Dr. Sýngmann had turned away to the window again: Strange that one should never tire of looking at sheep. Why should that be?

Long silence except for the whirring of my spool, which could just as well be a buzzing in the ears. The Doctor turned from the window and prepared to leave: an ageing giant worn out from living in mountain peaks and wading home through torrential rivers, his chest heavy, and perhaps with a pain at the heart. He stopped talking as the inventor of epagogics and his voice became gruff and brittle.

Dr. Godman Sýngmann: I'm going out to the hut to snatch a few hours' sleep before we start for the glacier. John, will you say a prayer with me?

Pastor Jón Prímus: I'd rather not, my friend. I'm completely away from all that sort of thing. Modern times brush their teeth instead of saying their prayers at night.

Dr. Godman Sýngmann: Perhaps it isn't right either. It just sort of occurred to me. Because we have both known Úa. Dandelion and honeybee, you say. That's just it, dandelion and honeybee. That's all there is to it. And yet I thought we could have said this prayer together.

Pastor Jón Prímus: What prayer?

Dr. Sýngmann: Oh, I don't know. Perhaps that thing by pastor Paul.

Pastor Jón: "Ever trusting"! How is it possible to remember that after having gone so far and been away so long?

Dr. Sýngmann: I don't know, John. Perhaps I'm a little tired. I hope you don't hold it against me, John.

Pastor Jón Prímus: I gave it up so long ago. The late pastor Jens of Setberg never said a prayer, but then he was a holy man and a soothsayer. God would burst out laughing if I started saying prayers.

Dr. Sýngmann: Once again forgive me, John. And let me

know if you need any trifling thing that is unobtainable here in Iceland. I'll buy it and send it to you by post.

Pastor Jón Prímus: That's a kind offer and it's just like you, Mundi, old friend. But I can easily let you have the money, you know. The trouble is I'm not short of anything. Still, it occurs to me that if you ever come across a good-quality horse-scratcher anywhere abroad, do buy it and send it to me by post. Here at home they have nothing but plain cow-scratchers.

Dr. Sýngmann: Horse-scratcher, yes, yes. I'll try to remember that, John. Good night, John. And you, my young friend, you who are about to launch out into the deep: launch out into the deep.

Exit Dr. Godman Sýngmann, closing the creaking door behind him.

28

The Glacier

When one is describing Christianity at Glacier one must never forget the glacier, at least not for long. Perhaps some of the undersigned's continuous reflections on this subject, as follows, are not entirely out of place even though they do not perhaps pertain to this particular day; but all other days have been this day at one time or another, just like those that are still to come.

This glacier is never like an ordinary mountain. As was said before, it is only a bulge and doesn't reach very high into the sky. It's as if this mountain has no point of view. It asserts nothing. It doesn't try to force anything upon anyone. It never importunes you. Skilled mountaineers come straight here to climb the mountain because it is one of the most famous mountains in the world, and when they see it they ask: Is that all there is to it? And they can't be bothered going up. In the mountain range that continues to the east of the glacier there are innumerable mountains as varied as people in a photograph; these mountains are not all-or-nothing like the glacier, but are endowed with details. Some are said to swell up and start booming when the wind is from the north. Some skilled mountaineers say that the glacier isn't interesting but that Helgrindur is interesting and the people should rather climb Helgrindur, which means the Gate of Hell.

It is often said of people with second sight that their soul leaves the body. That doesn't happen to the glacier. But the next time one looks at it, the body has left the glacier, and nothing remains except the soul clad in air. As the undersigned mentioned earlier in the report, the glacier is illuminated at certain times of the day by a special radiance and stands in a golden glow with a powerful aureole of rays, and everything becomes insignificant except it. Then it's as if the mountain is no longer taking part in the history of geology but has become ionic. Wasn't the fairy ram that Hnallþóra saw actually the glacier? A remarkable mountain. At night when the sun is off the mountains the glacier becomes a tranquil silhouette that rests in itself and breathes upon man and beast the word *never*, which perhaps means *always*. Come, waft of death.

29

Miracle Postponed

It must now be related that your emissary is roused from his sleep early in the morning, after having been witness the previous evening to the conversation that was cited above. There was a hammering with clenched fists on my door—not with the knuckles, however, but with the side of the hand, the way women use their fists for hitting.

Embi jumps out of bed in alarm, half-naked: What's wrong?

Woman's voice: The Angler cannot be woken up.

Embi: I'm a guest here. Better have a word with pastor Jón.

Woman: He was called away to Nes to break open a lock.

Embi: Is that Miss Hnallþóra?

Woman: My name is Mrs. Fína Jónsen from Hafnarfjörður and no damned Hnallþóra.

Embi: What do you want with me?

Mrs. Fína Jónsen: Well, the man's got to be woken up.

Embi: Wasn't there a twelve-tonner here last night?

Mrs. Fína Jónsen: Jódínus, you mean? To the best of my knowledge I've had him between my knees most of the night. I've got nothing more to say to that wretch. And besides he's now on his back underneath the truck and has started tinkering.

Embi: And the winter-pasture shepherds?

Mrs. Fína Jónsen: The ones with the hair and the beards? They're in fits of laughter out in the homefield beside the calf. The English chauffeur, he knows you're a bishop and he sent me to fetch you.

Embi: Where's the man from Langavatnsdalur? He's nearer to being a bishop than I.

Mrs. Fína Jónsen: Helgi of Torfhvalastaðir has been out looking for horses all night. There's no one around here in his right mind.

The professor's shiny black Imperial stands on the overgrown path to the church, gathering dew in the fog.

Your emissary had thought that Godman Sýngmann would be lying in his bed, seeing that he was to be woken up, but the professor had got no farther than the sitting room. He had not had time to take off his big jacket, managed no more than to loosen the collar of his shirt. The crumpled old hat lay in the middle of the floor as if it had been thrown, festooned with flies and colourful tin bait. The man had lowered himself onto a twin settee, had presumably felt a pain, and started to swallow tablets he had in his pockets, because on a small table by his side stood two open phials, the one containing yellow tablets, the other brown. He sat slumped with his head lolling to one side, his eyes screwed up and his mouth slack. The man was dead. In death, the wig had fallen off his head and lay on the floor.

The "chauffeur" turned out to be the man who saw to the housekeeping for the expedition. He greeted me and introduced himself as Mr. James Smith, the Butler. This butler wanted the corpse moved to the bedroom off the sitting room. In the country, the telephone doesn't open until 0800, so a doctor could not be contacted immediately in order to certify the death. The undersigned asked this butler if it would not be right to summon the professor's three colleagues.

Butler James Smith: Who are they?

When I had managed to make him understand whom I meant, he says: They're not asked. If they come in, I go out.

Embi: All the same, it would be a courtesy to talk to them!

Butler: On your head be it!

But it wasn't right to say that the winter-pasture shepherds were in fits of laughter; in point of fact they were out in the homefield doing morning exercises in accordance with hatha yoga, which consists of raising the god Kundalini who lives in the tailbone and reigns supreme over a man's life and soul if he is correctly tamed. The men alternately sat in Buddha postures or went down on their knees and bowed incessantly so low that they struck their foreheads on the ground, or lay flat, face-down; and this was what Mrs. Fína Jónsen had taken to be falling about in fits of laughter.

When these men heard what had happened, and that they were expected to carry their master's body a few paces from one room to another, Saknússemm II, who spoke on their behalf, said that he and his brothers took no account of death and would not lend a hand to the work that was required of them; that sort of thing wasn't in their sphere. This spokesman for the winter-pasture shepherds said it was high time their lord and master, Lord Maitreya, started attending to his work at home in that heaven where Buddha the fifth dwelt and where there was more to be done than here; he had now abandoned the carcass of an American businessman that he had been using for a while as a casing. The three of them, on the other hand, had undertaken this journey to this North Pole here for the purpose of raising from the dead a high female reincarnation who slept in the snow, and they would attend to no other work until that task was completed. For these men the most urgent need was to strengthen their omnipotence with that fire that lies hidden at the bottom of the spinal cavity in human beings, the snake-fire Kundalini. The lute-player for his part wanted to make up for the indifference that could be inferred from the pronouncement made by the leader, Saknússemm the Second, and began to mutter something, a bit feebly, in rather bad English mixed with Spanish phrases:

Señores, I suggest, *porque yo amo vosotros* that we shrink his head. We shrink it until it is as hard as rock and the size of a potato. Then we shall use it as a weathervane on the cathedral of the North Pole. Then the one who had it on loan and has now gone home to the fifth heaven can continue to talk to it, through it, and for it to us, *también muchas gracias.*

The sleeping master Epimenides rose smiling to his feet, turned his back, and took three steps away from the others. His garland lay on the grass. Nearly all the flowers in it were gone, and unfortunately there was little likelihood that new ones would grow in their place. Then he went down on his paws and rested his forehead on the ground.

Then something came to light that no one had noticed because of the morning's preoccupations—the glacier, which men from the four corners of the earth had been determined to climb that very morning, had vanished completely. Everything shrouded in fog right down to the farms, and Helgi of Torfh-valastaðir out in the fog looking for horses.

Jódínus Álfberg the poet: The Tycoon is dead, but he had already paid up. He paid well, because he was a Supertycoon. But now that Helgi of Torfhvalastaðir cannot find the horses and is himself lost and the glacier gone to the devil, what's the point of twelve tons and eighteen wheels? Kindly tell the English sheriff that Jódínus is now going off with the twelve-tonner and the scrubbing job and will come back when the weather clears up. Tell the sheriff that though I am not a gentleman but only an ordinary workingman and an Icelander and poet to boot, I don't cheat a dead man who has already paid.

One might add that this was one of those mornings when it's as if all the holes and rents in the world had been plugged and caulked, not even a chink for a miracle.

30

Four Widows or a Fourfold Madam

The undersigned was present at the doctor's examination of the body and translated the death certificate for the butler. As soon as that was over he composed four Xp-telegrams to New York, Sydney, London, and Buenos Aires. The telegrams were all addressed to the same addressee, "Mrs. Professor Dr. Godman Sýngmann," in the American style of giving titles to wives. Mr. Smith asked me to dispatch them by telegraph. The operator complained that the telegrams all seemed to be for the one person although the addresses specified different countries: the telegraph office doesn't send to the same addressee the same telegram from the same sender to many addresses. The text of the telegram was as follows: "Dr. Godman Sýngmann died last night stop heart attack stop kindly send instructions stop James Smith butler." The telegraph staff said they were taking the liberty of talking plain sense, and maintained that since the addressee appeared to be not an international company but rather the widow of the man whom the telegram described as being dead, then surely this woman could only be found at one place.

Conversation between the undersigned and Mr. Smith (hereinafter called "the butler" or even "the butler of the household"):

Embi: The telegraph staff refuse to send the same person the same telegram in four countries at once.

Butler: It will be paid.

Embi: I know nothing of the marital status of the deceased nor does it concern me much. But I thought I caught a hint that Dr. Sýngmann was a widower. Who is the woman who has these four addresses, if I may ask?

Butler: That is my problem.

Embi: I am telling you the regulations of the telegraph office.

Butler: It so happens that I am the butler of this household.

Embi: I am the emissary of the Bishop of Iceland.

Butler: Bad luck. However, the telegrams I have signed are my own responsibility.

Embi: Though a special case like this is outside my scope, there is no hiding the fact that we are not indifferent to what we bury here. It's not as if we are piling a cairn over a horse. Judging by your telegrams, Dr. Godman Sýngmann seems to have been a somewhat ubiquitously married man. Though this doesn't concern me directly, it is the custom here in Iceland, when strangers die and are buried, to inquire about their age, address, nationality, and marital status.

Butler: Strangers? What are you talking about? This is one of the greatest men in the world.

Embi: Leave that aside for the moment. To revert to the telegrams: if this address is the name of a firm that has branches in many countries, that would be a different story. But why then doesn't it have either "Limited" or "Incorporated" at the end? If, on the other hand, the man had four wives as the telegrams imply, I would think that none of these women is a lawful party to this case, but that they must live separately somewhere behind lock and key. In all the countries that are named in the telegrams, polygamy is a major crime.

Butler: Will you have these telegrams sent or not, sir?

The bishop's emissary advised the man to talk to the management of the telegraph office, and the upshot was that the telegrams were sent.

31

Your New Instructions, and a Work-Report

Pastor Jón the locksmith asks me not to leave until everything has been attended to. The clergyman says yet again that the responsibility of the office weighs heavily upon him. He says he hopes that aeroplanes from the four corners of the earth would arrive soon to quarter Mundi's carcass and remove the parts each to its own continent. Axlar-Björn the highwayman, the most famous man ever known at Glacier, was buried under three cairns, says the parish pastor, and likewise he has heard that kings of the Ming dynasty were each laid to rest in twelve mausoleums.

The day wears on without replies being received from the four widows. The butler drives off to do some shopping in the Imperial limousine; the twelve-tonner with Jódínus the poet follows like a dog. Pastor Jón and I stay behind and await events, and I keep an eye on the winter-pasture shepherds so that they don't take the head off the corpse and shrink it. I say I'm going south because my mission here is finished, and this makes pastor Jón a little depressed, until he gets the idea of inviting me out to the shed, and says that an old woman at Nes had given him some smoked brisket. He cut thick slices from it and we ate it raw and it was a wonderful delicacy and besides I was starving. He put the kettle on and boiled his strong kettle-coffee, and there was plenty of rye bread and butter and moreover dried halibut for all of £20 sterling. Eventually a telegram arrived and we both held our breaths in suspense over what the fourfold woman of the world would say.

But this was a telegram from your Grace the Bishop of Iceland—to me. Attached herewith:

"On behalf of the Ministry of Ecclesiastical Affairs kindly supervise funeral of Australian engineer of Icelandic origin who died at Glacier this morning, to be buried there according to cabled request received this minute from Mowitz & Cattleweight Ltd., Solicitors & Brokers, Securities Corporation London W. C., etc., as follows: Mr. Sýngmann of Australia died in Iceland this morning. Kindly bury the man immediately. Attestations of responsible authority requested. Costs payable in this London office. End quote. Delegate you responsibility for lawful preparation and execution of desired ceremony. Those officials concerned, in addition to foreign representatives, will be attending. Bishop of Iceland."

Embi: It's probably best to start putting windowpanes in the church, pastor Jón.

Pastor Jón: Oh, the church hasn't any funds left.

Embi: The London people will pay.

Pastor Jón: What difference would it make to them to take him away to London? After that they could take him to Australia, now that they reckon he belongs there. Or what do his three colleagues have to say?

Embi: They want to shrink his head. That's the only suggestion they have to make. Better pay no attention to them.

Pastor Jón: Perhaps you would like to bury him yourself?

Embi: What gives you that idea! I am not ordained. I cannot even sprinkle earth, by law. On the other hand I have my instructions here in a confirmed telegram from the bishop. They state clearly and unmistakably that I am responsible for the lawful execution of this business. As far as I can see, it is you, the parish pastor, and none other, who is the responsible authority concerned.

Pastor Jón: Don't you think it at all comical to be burying people from my church? In my churchyard?

Embi waves the telegram: Here are my instructions!

Pastor Jón: It so happens that I haven't the stomach to hold a funeral sermon over this man. We were rivals in love. He was such a magician that he changed our sweetheart into a fish.

Evening. The butler arrives from the south in the Imperial and Jódínus trundles along behind with the coffin in the twelve-tonner and no other cargo except for Mrs. Fína Jónsen in the front seat. There is also a builder in tow, whose task is to see what needs to be done to improve the church; he says that carpenters will be sent tomorrow. The parish pastor starts looking for a crowbar, because now the windows are to be opened up again; furthermore, the bars are to be torn from the door— and he having nailed them in place so carefully yesterday after the bishop's emissary had made his inspection. Mrs. Fína Jónsen waits outside with the scrubbing brush, and now the way into the church is open. It is forty-eight centimetres up to the threshold, as was stated earlier in this report, but Mrs. Fína Jónsen says it doesn't matter, she can easily take thresholds of this size in her stride. But in this church neither the scrubbing brush nor soap were of any avail, not even a bristle broom; instead, Jódínus says he will fetch a man with a shovel tomorrow. The builder takes notes, promises to come with a gang tomorrow as well, and drives off home.

The body had to be coffined. We carried the coffin into the bungalow. The winter-pasture shepherds had lain down to rest on the veranda under the portico, where it doesn't rain; it is not their custom to enter human dwellings except in wild weather, cf. foxes have their dens, etc. They peer out from their sleeping bags without saying good evening, and curl up under cover again. We pushed the furniture aside in the sitting room and stacked some of it against the walls, then set up the bier in the middle of the floor. Mrs. Fína Jónsen washed the body where it lay on the bed, and we lifted it as and when required to ease her task; it was very stiff. The knee-joints, which had in fact been indistinct in life, were solid as blocks of ice. Mrs. F. J. produced a shroud from her bag and says, I sewed this from material for a nightdress I had intended for myself. Then we dressed the body. When that was done the woman says Such is life, meaning that a nightdress she had intended for herself was now being used for the greatest angler in the world. After that we carried the body into the sitting room and laid it in the coffin and the undersigned was allowed to support this famous man's head. It was quite an effort to cross the arms over his breast. Now he lies there. His face was no longer a mottled blue, but brown from old suns in hot countries. Then the following exchange takes place:

Butler: Is no one here saying a prayer?

Pastor Jón Prímus, rather weakly: Oh, praying, I've been away from it so long.

Embi to the butler: You are the butler.

Then the butler started to mutter an English prayer in an undertone, but very fast, so that the undersigned could hardly tell whether it was the Lord's Prayer or "It's a Long Way to Tipperary." Your emissary thought pastor Jón looked as if the prayer made his skin crawl. Mrs. Fína Jónsen looked at the men as if to ask if that was all they proposed to contribute. It seemed so. So the woman produced an old hymnbook, rather worn but with gilt edges, and tucked it inside on the dead man's breast. She made the sign of the cross over the face, expertly, first with a perfectly straight movement of the hand up and down, thereby delineating the upright, then forming the crossbar with a flat hand, the palm downwards. Finally she spread a veil over the man's face, saying: May the Lord be praised for your life.

That was all, and nothing more was needed, really. Pastor Jón said that Miss Hnallþóra was offering coffee and cakes over in the parsonage.

32

Night Vigil

At your request I shall prolong my stay here for those days while Dr. Godman Sýngmann's body lies on the bier, although I do not dare to take responsibility for anything that might happen here. Incalculable agents are involved in this. However, I promise to do everything in my power to prevent the body being taken up onto the glacier, its head removed and shrunk, etc.

I have noticed that the Ministry of Ecclesiastical Affairs is cooperating with the deceased's butler, Mr. Smith, an Englishman, as well as his Icelandic errand-boy in the district, Jódínus Álfberg. It is presumably through this cooperation that windowpanes have been put in the church, the roof mended, and so on. The undersigned also wishes to note, with gratitude, that the church has been completely mucked out and the doors repaired a little, although they have not been entirely cured of the creaking. There have been some minor repairs around the altar. I also think it of importance that a set of steps, 48 cm high, has been placed against the church door so that most parishioners who are reasonably hale and of normal length of leg and mobility now have the opportunity of achieving entry to God's house at Glacier—if the church door isn't nailed up again sooner than expected. In addition a stepladder was placed in the bell tower, so that now one can scramble up and ring the bell.

Concerning the altarpiece already mentioned in this report, I would point out that I have prevented the old paintings on it from being scrubbed with caustic soda with the kind of scrubbing brush that Hafnarfjörður people use for scouring the scales off haddock. Perhaps it would be possible to clean the altarpiece with specially prepared materials if a qualified expert could be found for the task.

As regards the boards from the pulpit, which had previously been tied together in a bundle, and also a valuable chandelier in German baroque style that was lying on the floor in 133 parts, I think it likely that these items were cleared by the shovel when the church was mucked out, and the undersigned wasn't quick enough to lay hands on them.

The three winter-pasture shepherds are still here, settled on the veranda of the bungalow, and say they will be delayed in their task because of the fog: with that done, the "butler of the household" will see to their passage home.

These people have been asked to what denomination Dr. Godman Sýngmann had adhered; and furthermore, if it were likely that a representative of the church in question would want to travel to Iceland and conduct the funeral if the parish pastor here pleaded difficulty, on grounds of faith, in having Lutherans involved in the business.

These people are not always agreeable in their replies. They say of Dr. Sýngmann's body that this is the carcass of an international businessman; their master had had this container on loan. Skip it! Their master had no religion. He was himself Buddha. Buddha frequently pops down here to earth on important business without being reincarnated; this time he came to put into effect a special revelation in six volumes and to carry out a rather urgent resurrection mystery. The revelation was accomplished, but the miracle will be performed as soon as the rain stops. The Lord himself has now discarded his coarse container and has gone home to his heaven. From there he will come in a reincarnated image as the fifth Buddha after about three thousand years or so to redeem the world and complete the work of deliverance he has previously instituted in books and miracles.

The undersigned cannot judge whether this doctrine is Buddhism any more than anything else. The one certain thing is that I recognise bits of it although I am not a Buddhist. The undersigned is not trying to explain anything nor add anything, but in my judgement the aforementioned body is, according to this doctrine, entitled to be buried in accordance with universal Christian faith with any necessary adjustments. It's another matter that one of the winter-pasture shepherds, the lute-player, is obviously descended from the headhunters of South America, and has suggested obtaining Dr. Sýngmann's head for shrinking.

I have impressed upon Mr. Smith the necessity of keeping careful vigil over the body, on behalf of Messrs. Mowitz & Cattleweight Inc., Solicitors & Brokers, etc., and I entrust him with the responsibility for it while the body is lying in the bungalow; but as soon as the church is in order, the undersigned will keep vigil over the body on behalf of the Ministry of Ecclesiastical

Affairs in accordance with instructions and by agreement with the parish pastor.

The evening before the funeral. The carpenters have gone and the grave-diggers have been at work. The coffin has been moved into the church. Only one thing is still uncertain regarding this funeral, and that is whether it will take place. Pastor Jón Prímus has not yet given his unequivocal assent; he vanished this morning before people were up, and has not been seen all day. Phone calls have been made in vain all over the district.

Night; darkness and drizzle. The winter-pasture shepherds are asleep on the veranda of the bungalow under the portico. The body is in its place and the coffin open at the head, and the lid will not be completely closed before the proper authorities have compared it with their documents. I decide to lie down for an hour and forget my worries, in the hope that the Creator will somehow or other find a way out of the morning's difficulties.

I have hardly been in bed for more than a minute when I hear fugitive footsteps on the farmhouse paving—are the winter-pasture shepherds now on the move with the head? But when I went out to investigate, it turned out to be sheep on the run; they announced themselves by bleating. The night was wet and heavy. It was the kind of rain that makes the whole body feel cold regardless of the temperature: rain of the soul. I lay down again, exhausted by worries that were demonstrably premature. This time I fell into a doze, but almost at once a nightmare began. I seemed to think I had forgotten to put out the candle at the coffin's head, and now the candle had fallen to the floor and blue flames like some sort of floating matter were beginning to flood the church floor. I put my shoes on again in a trice and rushed out to the church. But there had never been any candle, of course, far less a light. In my doze there had come to my mind vague recollections of chiaroscuro paintings of vigils with the gleam of a candle at the feet of the deceased.

It is dark in the church, to be sure, despite the new window-panes; but it never gets so dark at night between May and June that one cannot see the glimmer of thick moisture on grass that is sprouting outside.

The altarpiece is nonetheless darker than ever before. I was wondering whether it had not been interfering on my part to forbid Mrs. Fína Jónsen to treat this ancient art with a scrubbing brush and that powerful caustic soda; hadn't she undertaken the whole thing at hourly rates? Somehow I felt as if these pictures looked at me with heavy accusation from deep within their silent ruin, and it could be that they were right and that it was wrong to invent a cleaning polish to bring out what has disappeared.

I had now got out of bed twice. I did not think it worth the trouble to go to bed a third time. The winter-pasture shepherds think they are at the North Pole, and that this is the cathedral there. This was perhaps exaggerated, in a way, but still there is something afoot here, like walrus ghosts, and my mind is full of untimely thoughts; I am only twenty-five years old, after all. I sat down at the foot of the bier and dozed off with my chin on my chest.

There was a diabolical squealing in the wretched hinges, and I woke up again. Someone was entering the church: pastor Jón Prímus. He half-dragged himself through the door. Seemed to be all in. Soaked to the skin, poor man. Nor was his footwear a pretty sight after wading through mud and ferrous water. I was sure I was dreaming, but said good morning nonetheless to be on the safe side.

Pastor Jón Prímus: Good morning.

Embi: I see you have been out for a stroll, pastor Jón. Where did you land in such a mess?

Pastor Jón Prímus: Here at Glacier we have the most celebrated mineral springs in the world. I landed in them.

He sat down on the altar rail and took off one of his shoes and then the sock, and then he said: I have turned my ankle slightly; I want to see if it is swollen. He rubbed his ankle and remarked: Probably a little suffused with blood; and he recited a verse from the Psalms of David:

"I will not reprove thee for thy sacrifices, because thy burnt offerings are always before mine eyes; for every beast of the forest is mine; and the cattle upon a thousand hills; all the fowls do I know; the lilies of the field are with me."

With these words he put on his wet sock again and the muddy shoe: I had better say hello to Mundi now, he said.

Embi: Thank God you turned up to bury the man tomorrow morning, pastor Jón.

Pastor Jón Prímus: Definitely not one damned person do I bury! Have you got a match?

The lid was not quite closed, the coffin was open at the head as was said earlier. We lifted the veil and illuminated the face with the match. The face had an expression of profound remoteness. Whoever gazed upon it must look forward to this one day, the first day after dying.

I have accounted for the circumstance whereby I stood at the side of pastor Jón Prímus in this remarkable church and we contemplated the expression of farthest human remoteness. The match went out.

Pastor Jón Prímus: Strange that such a tube should have been concerning himself with how to run the Creation.

The undersigned was thinking of asking the parish pastor whether he had said tube or type, but could not be bothered to follow it up, and anyway it did not matter. Actually, he undoubtedly said tube. I laid the veil over the face again.

33

The Mourners and
Their Solace

It was intimated to all those concerned that the funeral of Dr.
Godman Sýngmann would take place on May 19 at eleven
o'clock. At the appointed time, another six black limousines
joined the deceased's Imperial, which was already there. Out of
these luxurious official cars stepped a number of men dressed
in black. The party of mourners wasn't very large, certainly, but
it was solemn and impressive. Here is a list of those present
(attendants, chauffeurs, and office staff not included):

Mr. Christie, British Consul-General for Iceland;

Mr. Smith, Dr. Sýngmann's butler;

Mr. David, an official of the United States Embassy;

An English emissary of the firm of Messrs. Mowitz & Cattleweight Ltd., Securities Corporation, Solicitors & Brokers,
London W. C., etc;

The sheriff of Snæfells County;

A representative of the Ministry of Justice;

An emissary of the bishop (the undersigned);

Jódínus Álfberg, poet, the deceased's local representative, author of the Palisander Lay;

Choir (consisting of Tumi Jónsen the parish clerk and two other worthies, all very advanced in years);

Mrs. Fína Jónsen, widow, from Hafnarfjörður, mentioned above in the report, who supplied the veil, etc.

Missing, on the other hand, are the four widows of the deceased, i.e., the women who bore his name in Buenos Aires, Sydney, London, and New York; they had, however, been sent telegrams.

From the Langvetningur the parish pastor has received the following telegram, datelined north in Húnavatns County: Regret cannot make burial. Hope to arrive for resurrection. Have sold the horses. Kind regards. Helgi of Torfhvalastaðir.

We shall only touch lightly here upon the lengthy arguments that were used on pastor Jón Prímus right up to the last moment, so reluctant was the pastor to conduct this ceremony, or rather, so difficult was it to nag him into it. He said he had a sore foot and had caught a chill—something in that. Hadn't had time to sleep for three days and nights because of onerous official duties—arguable. No paper to be found in the house on which to write funeral sermons, and no time for writing, and besides he had forgotten how to write—pretexts.

The undersigned pointed out that nothing was required of a pastor except that he intimate in church at the dead man's bier his date of birth and date of death and thereafter say some little prayer or other, even if it were only the Lord's Prayer; and finally sprinkle the State's three spadefuls of earth with the statutory innocent phrases, Earth to earth, etc., as is the custom.

Pastor Jón Prímus: That's not so innocent as it looks. It derives from those scholastics. They were always doing their utmost to falsify Aristotle, though he was quite bad enough already. They tried to feed the fables with yet more fables, such as that the primary elements of matter first disintegrate and then reassemble again in order to resurrect. They lied so fast in the Middle Ages they hadn't even time to hiccup.

Embi: In the Middle Ages it was also the custom to write down a formula on a piece of paper and lay it against a sore, and then it healed. For internal ailments a mixture was prepared and given to a dog belonging to the man who was sick, and he would then recover. When I was a little boy I cured a wart I had by sticking a tongue-bone into a wall.

Pastor Jón Prímus: Cold water for me.

Embi: But sometimes also nice and hot, with plenty of coffee in it.

Now pastor Jón Prímus laughed. Philosophy and theology have no effect on him, much less plain common sense. Impossible to convince this man by arguments. But humour he always listens to, even though it be ill humour. A typical Icelander, perhaps. Sometimes your emissary would have given a lot, however, to be able to see the world from the standpoint of pastor Jón Prímus.

Embi, when pastor Jón has stopped laughing: There will be no one else here except foreign and home officials, and their business is to make a report. If they don't see a pastor, there will be no report—no funeral, no nothing, and everything ending up in fuss and bother, diplomatic action, and international complications all over the world. You and I would both be put in jail, perhaps.

Dignified gentlemen stood stiffly around the coffin in the

middle of the church and had begun to wait. The choristers on the other hand had been allotted seats on account of their age, and told not to stand up until they were given the signal to start singing. Pastor Jón entered the church at 1113 hours. He did not close the door behind him, and the church stood open. Birds flew past the door. A yellow-striped stray cat sat on a grave and longed for breakfast, but the breakfast sang its trilling song up on the church gable. There was fog along the mountain ridges, but the weather passed for dry down here.

The pastor's cassock must originally have been made for a much smaller clergyman than pastor Jón Prímus—lost property, perhaps—or else excessively shrunk: it was far too tight for him. This cassock was multicoloured, as if it had lain out in the open for a few years, for the most part under snow; and full of holes as if insects had been at work there, perhaps also mice. The pastor walked nonchalantly straight to the coffin, completely unaffected by the presence of solemn mourners, and halted at the left side of the head of the coffin. That is not where a pastor ought to stand, but perhaps pastor Jón thought he was going to shoe a horse. He stood for a while and looked straight out of the open door, a little pensive, and raised his hand to his wolf-grey mane and scratched his head, and tried to remember something; then he wiped his face hard as if he were squeezing a rubber mask. Finally he produced his manual from his cassock pocket, but had then forgotten his spectacles.

He lifted the book to his nose and squinted at it, but had difficulty in finding anything suitable to read. He became a little anxious as he hunted through the book. Until now I had thought that pastor Jón was the last man to get flustered. But it hardly escaped those present that this parish pastor didn't feel at home in a cassock. I myself felt I was now seeing pastor Jón

Prímus for the first time not at play. The British Consul leaned across to the undersigned and asked in a whisper on behalf of Her Majesty if it were quite definite that this man believed in God.

Embi: Yes.

Now pastor Jón finds near the back of the book the formulas that are prescribed for the burial of so-called "adult persons" who do not get a special funeral sermon: this normally refers to paupers and thieves or else drownings and bodies that have been washed ashore from shipwrecks. There you find, *inter alia*, the words: Lord, thou makest man return to dust. But pastor Jón Prímus shakes his head and skips over that as well. When he has dipped into various places and tasted the occasional word here and there, he finally reaches a passage and stops; he had no doubt forgotten it; he now starts examining this passage, and weighs and assesses each word to himself, though everyone could easily hear him, and then he reads aloud: "Because no one of us lives for himself and no one dies for himself. For if we live, then we live for the Lord; and if we die, then we die for the Lord. Therefore whether we live or die we belong to the Lord."

Pastor Jón Prímus to himself: That's rather good.

With that he thrust the manual into his cassock pocket, turned towards the coffin, and said:

That was the formula, Mundi. I was trying to get you to understand it, but it didn't work out; actually it did not matter. We cannot get round this formula anyway. It's easy to prove that the formula is wrong, but it is at least so right that the world came into existence. But it is a waste of words to try to impute to the Creator democratic ideas or social virtues; or to think that one can move Him with weeping and wailing, and persuade Him with logic and legal quibbles. Nothing is so pointless as words. The late pastor Jens of Setberg knew all this and more besides. But he also knew that the formula is kept in a locker. The rest comes by itself. The Creation, which includes you and me, we are in the formula, this very formula I have just been reading; and there is no way out of it. Because no one lives for himself and so on; and whether we live or die, we and so on.

You are annoyed that demons should govern the world and that consequently there is only one virtue that is taken seriously by the newspapers: killings.

You said they had discovered a machine to destroy everything that draws breath on earth; they were now trying to agree on a method of accomplishing this task quickly and cleanly; preferably while having a cocktail. They are trying to break out of the formula, poor wretches. Who can blame them for that? Who has never wanted to do that?

Many consider the human being to be the most useless animal on earth or even the lowest stage of evolution in all the universe put together, and that it is more than high time to wipe this creature out, like the mammoth in the tundras. We once knew a war maiden, you and I. There was only one word ever found for her: Úa. So wonderful was this creation that it's no exaggeration to say that she was completely unbearable; indeed I think that we two helped one another to destroy her, and yet perhaps she is still alive. There was never anything like her.

Like all great rationalists you believed in things that were twice as incredible as theology. I bid you welcome to this poor parish at Glacier to be united with the power-generator of the Creation and the intelligences that dwell on the planets of the galaxies. It was a good idea to summon to your assistance people who have the law of determinants in their power and thereby communion with life-giving beings in infinite space. I can well understand that such people do not enter such a poor church as mine. I bow my head before your honourable mourners, my dear Mundi, who have come here from distant places to take part in a requiem service.

In conclusion I, as the local pastor, thank you for having participated in carrying the Creation on your shoulders alongside me. This parish at Glacier is actually a good living, but it is a little difficult sometimes, especially for horses. I am always trying to wring out some hay-sweepings here and there to feed to them in hard weather. And yet horses out in the open are always full of pranks and start kicking up their heels and boxing and uttering mating cries, however badly they are being treated: and one never knows whether they are in earnest or not; yes, one can learn much from these creatures in a horse-torturing society such as this. Of the snow bunting I have nothing to add to what I said the other day to a young man who was looking for truth: if there is an Almighty in the heavens, it is to be found in the snow bunting. Whatever happens, the snow bunting survives; no sooner have the blizzards abated than it has started courting. And the lilies of the field, they toil not; neither do they spin. I might also mention the brightly coloured small birds of the South Sea islands. One thing is certain; we need have nothing to fear, honourable mourners, because whether we live or die, it so happens that we have the same God as the Mohammedans in the desert—and of Him the late pastor Jens of Setberg said: Allah is great. (Tape-recorded.)

34

Extra Day at Glacier

I wake up well rested.

Last night I went to bed in the belief that now my mission was concluded and that Christianity at Glacier was more or less committed to paper. The death of Prof. Dr. Godman Sýngmann was also successfully settled, and with that I had once again packed my things. It is a long time since I have slept so soundly. Estimated time of departure from here the same as before (1145 hours).

It was not until I had finished shaving that I see that a slip of paper has been eased in between doorpost and door: it lies on the floor just inside the threshold.

"Three o'clock at night. Dear kind Mr. Emissary. Will need the church this evening as we agreed, but didn't have the heart to wake you about it in the middle of the night. We're setting off up the glacier early at daybreak, and hope to be back by bedtime tonight with a little luggage, Jódínus and I and three World Teachers plus truck, caterpillar tractor, and jeep since my horses have probably been made into soup up north by now. Unfortunately motor engines are not conducive to the law of determinants. But now we have to get a move on because our determinanters are leaving and dry weather is forecast and good visibility on the glacier. Despite the machinery, diexelixis will conquer dysexelixis, *i* will conquer *y*, that's what we believe. Then everything will go well. The world will then become whole. And I will buy big horses, Helgi."

Aha, says the undersigned, this was only to be expected, I suppose! Or had I been so naive as to imagine that a sunny-smiling world-haggler like the parish officer from Torfhvalastaðir would ever throw in the towel? Obviously such men don't stop until diexelixis has conquered dysexelixis. Now God's House stands as it were defenceless and wide open for every crank there is, with pastor Jón traipsing about the countryside again in the discharge of the onerous duties of his office as usual.

So it follows that I must once again stay on here until evening and then try with episcopal backing and clerical authority to defend the church against these redeemers.

Instead of now driving home after a job well done, I wandered about the farmstead on my own as the day went by, or lay at the edge of the cliff listening to the birds, and fell asleep. Miss Hnallþóra has surely gone away on a journey; I wouldn't be surprised if she had overstrained herself at the baking, since yesterday she had to provide coffee and cakes for the Great Powers, the emissary of world capitalism from London, and many other good men; perhaps she has gone away to try to recover.

The undersigned set off along the main road in search of the metropolis that is clearly marked on the map and lies, according to the scale, about five kilometres ahead; but the road is so twisting and climbs up and down so many glacier moraines that I was five hours all told on the road there and back.

The metropolis proved to consist of three farmsteads, standing scattered at the frontier where the cliffs end and the low-lying shore begins. In the cellar of one of the farms there was a tiny shop, and when I finally got hold of the housewife she sold me from the shop's foodstocks some stale chocolate and tinned asparagus; and of course the celebrated Prince Polo biscuits, the only gastronomic luxury that Icelanders have allowed themselves since they became a wealthy nation. In the mouth this delicacy is not unlike the pumice one can find in dried-up riverbeds from the glacier, except for a little extra sweetness of taste that would make normal pumice rather more inedible than ever. This titbit the undersigned forced down like raw train oil, as it says in the poem about Ásmunder of Rembihnútur, for hunger was pressing hard. I sat on a grassy bank by the main road where a little brook ran past, and I had the brook along with the asparagus for dessert. The water was such that I understood at last pastor Jón Prímus's cold water doctrine, which says that it's quite enough to have one doctrine but not to practise it unless one is thirsty.

If I have forgotten to write about the weather. That is soon remedied: it has cleared up. A cloudless day. The glacier reigns snowy-white and stock-still over an unordained priestling who sits on a grassy bank by a brook chewing Prince Polo biscuits, and is mentally arming himself to defend the revelation, the faith, and God's Christianity against campers, miracle makers, horse traders, and twelve-tonner people. A good day. The day one did not lose one's faith. How precisely symmetrical the glacier is as it lies mirrored in the water of Bárðarlaug.

35

Yet Another Disputation about the Same Thing

Embi to farmer Helgi of Torfhvalastaðir in Langavatnsdalur, late that evening: For as long as I remain here at this church as the emissary of the bishop I shall not depart from what I said the other day: first we see what is in the box, and not until then do we take any decision on whether the contents should be afforded ecclesiastical treatment or not.

Langvetningur: My teacher, who is closer to me now than ever before—he attached great importance to the box getting epagogic treatment.

Embi: If you don't mind, this is a Christian church.

Langvetningur: Though I believe in cosmobiology, along with astrochemistry, biotelekinesis, and all that, it's not because my mentor omitted to point out in his writings that the church is the home of the soul. Who would deny that the church is the horse-fair of the soul?

Embi: Aha! When you go to a horse-fair, don't you behave according to the rules of the horse-fair? You would scarcely buy a horse unseen. We don't either.

Langvetningur: My teacher summoned here three spirits who are of the opinion—and I think they have a point—that he himself kindled them into human form, just as the Finns once kindled Eyvindur Kinnrifa to life, according to Snorri Sturluson in *Heimskringla*. This harmony-group has come here in order to start a new era in biology. You know as well as I that the rays of the galaxies are refracted in the glacier. Our bishop ought to give due consideration to our request that the soul be allowed to wake up and resurrect in a church.

Embi: I am asking what is in the box. Nothing else matters.

The poet Jódínus joins in the conversation, using the formal *you*: Though we are only ordinary people, mate, we have leave to talk, isn't that so? We have the World Redeemers with us. Gag us if you dare.

Langvetningur: May a farmer and horseman say a word on behalf of his mentor who lives on the planets of the galaxies though he is closer to us than we ourselves to ourselves, and looks from there with the eyes of the All-thinking and All-doing upon everything that happens in time?

Embi: Should we not rather break open the box and have a look inside and use our own eyes as far as they go? After that we can discuss the matter.

Farmer Helgi of Torfhvalastaðir was by God's grace such a master at haggling over horses and bargaining over prices that his face with its space spectacles glowed in the darkness; no light was needed even at midnight when he was present, at least at this time of year. Our eyes, what are they? A legacy from the days of the monsters, the Reptile Age; relics of the shape of the leaping-lizard called Tyrannosaurus Rex, which weighed twenty tons and reared its hideous head twelve metres in the air: from that head do our eyes derive; for that reason we still lie in the prison of earthly vision from the Mesozoic era; with such eyes nothing can be perceived other than the world of this terrible creature. But, my dear bishop, there is one eye that sees: the eye that dwells deepest in universal space. That is the eye we are to meet tonight.

Jódínus takes a pull at his pocket-bottle and turns to me: Though Helgi and I are only Icelanders, we are poets all the same and stand above the world, though that isn't saying much. And though I'm no more than twelve tons fully laden compared with the big newt that Helgi mentioned, which was twenty tons, I was all the same entrusted with a box by a man who was perhaps as almighty as you, mate, and all you bishops. There you are, here it is; now show you aren't afraid.

36

A Geophysical Drop, and So On

A strange sound—whence came this music, which was scarcely music at all? The undersigned is standing out on the farmhouse paving in the night stillness—he thinks it safer to hang around until it's quite certain that these men have lost the desire to go to church. Though I have in fact forbidden them the church as matters stand, I thought it rather perverse of them not to suggest I should be present when the lid of the box was opened. Here's hoping I haven't offended these gentlemen. So I sat down on the church step as if to look after the church, and the step still smells of new-sawn wood; then I hear this faint music coming from around the corner. The semitransparent silhouette of the glacier now looms against the sky as it listens there and waits in the stillness of the night.

This music was like a drop that falls with three different notes, like the drops in a remote cavern. Silence in between.

But the silence is of varying length and the note depends on how much the drop has gathered into itself by the time it falls from the rocky vault in the darkness. This musical drop is unique and self-sufficient in the universe while it is wearing a hole in the stone; and no ear nearby, of course. This is music in the same way as eternity is genuine in a shrunken human head. The music with which we are familiar is a gigantic monument-making inspired by national festival tendencies and pontifical mass and other deafening celebrations of despair in the style of the Ninth Symphony, but is it genuine? One can say of this drop, as a poet once elegised the shortest member of parliament: There wasn't much material went into you, but what there was rang true. This lowly headhunter and lute-player from the Andes who has been playing for the calf at Glacier for a while—is he, when all is said and done, the one who plays the music of the absolute?

The Langvetningur, the twelve-tonner man, and the leader of the winter-pasture shepherds (who reads books, unfortunately)—these three carried the box between them past the church door where your emissary sat perched on the step; then they went round the corner. The undersigned stood up and strolled along behind it, whatever it was.

Embi: I prefer to be at hand even though I gather I am not invited—in case anything turns up that concerns Christianity.

The common man Jódínus says that "such a person," i.e., the undersigned, doesn't deserve to be called an Icelander because Icelanders have raised ghosts since time immemorial; they learned it from the Finns. Helgi of Torfhvalastaðir on the other hand says he is glad the bishop is so gracious as to have his proxy present as a witness to a consubstantiation such as Lutherans preach (if only halfheartedly) in the Communion service, but which every twopenny priest in popedom carries out in the Roman Catholic mass every day of the year, as casually as drinking water.

I was allowed onto the veranda of the bungalow under the portico. The moon was in the second quarter.

The sleeper Epimenides squatted on his haunches and smiled from the darkness, and sometimes there came a blue-green flash from his pupils, as in an animal. He had fastened some scurvy grass and crowberry heather in his garland, and now looked more like the gods than ever.

The Drop sat kneeling and touched his lute with long pauses in between searching for the note that can only be sought far back in geophysics. It has been proved that there was a dry spell on earth once for 200 million years. Not a drop from the sky. No life possible. Yet the idea of water, which is the idea of life, continued to live in the deserts of the earth. Perhaps this lute-player had captured a note of the drop that went on falling in remote caverns of the Andes for 200 million years. Let us hope and pray that the music of the absolute is not just yet another variant of the Anglo-Saxon antimusic that blares out from the ghetto blasters of the world night and day.

The one with the name Saknússemm the Second, who might unfortunately be a professor in Los Angeles, I suspect—he was trying to adopt sacred postures like Buddha, and used his poncho-blanket to conceal his obvious stiffness in Buddhism; he put on a wretched hat and pulled it down to his eyebrows. Behind him is the entrance to the bungalow, sealed by the sheriff while the legal heirs to the building have not been found anywhere in the world; I understand that the winter-pasture shepherds are no longer allowed to lay their heads anywhere now.

For a long time it was as if nothing would happen. Are they

going to sit like that, each one separate and without communication with one another, without having a ceremony or making any attempt to inspire each other, like three peering cats sitting below a wall without even caterwauling, never mind singing a hymn? But what if a mouse now emerged? Are they going to leave it to the Icelanders alone to lay bare the secrets of the universe? Or does the law of determinants consist of waiting passively for this strange thing that definitely exists and that governs infinity in time and space? Soon, however, our compatriots had begun to wield the crowbar.

The wooden box that had guarded its contents against the glacier snows for three years looked to be about a metre long, about 25 cm in width, and about the same thickness—is there a child inside it or what? Perhaps only one leg, a kind of *pars pro toto*? Or else a chopped-up body like the youngsters whom Saint Nicholas of Bari of blessed memory raised from the brine-tub? The box was solidly made but the wood had got wet through after the box was removed from the glacier frost and had now for a few hours been in an air temperature of circa twelve degrees. But when the boards had been prised open, they proved to be merely an outer covering. Inside there was a container made of light-coloured metal, which looked like silver that is beginning to tarnish, but turned out to be zinc; this metal has a blue-white, rather shell-grey colour called zinc-white, which is used for coating palisander walls in kitchens.

The zinc container now lies on the veranda and they are about to remove the lid. The undersigned could no longer keep silent at this point.

Embi in English: Is no one going to say anything, or what? Isn't it appropriate to recite something appropriate when there is a resurrection from the dead going on?

After a good while the following reply came from under the hat of Saknússemm the Second: Lord Maitreya raised the three of us from nothing and not a word was spoken then.

Whatever Lord Maitreya does, I thought it indefensible that farmer Helgi the Langvetningur of Torfhvalastaðir should not say something since the winter-pasture shepherds shrank from it.

Embi to farmer Helgi: Aren't you going to say something, man?

After a little pause the farmer went to the balustrade against the semitransparent silhouette of the glacier, gold-rimmed by the moon. He raised his arms and lifted his face with its spectacles towards the galaxies and started to talk to his master, mentor, and Doctor in the jargon they were wont to use with one another: The life you asked to await you in this container until you kindled it anew with bioinduction with the help of the law of determinants: that moment has now come when you make it step forth reincarnated in astrochemical perfection and thereby change the biology of the earth. Your employees and determinanters will now take the lid off this shrine—

37

The Veranda, Continued: Night

Good evening.

Who is this mysterious good-evening-bidder who speaks thus at this time of day? The radio or what?

On the veranda in our midst there stands a woman. She is perhaps fully middle-aged, comely, wearing a classic burberry coat and a pale blue slouch hat of hide or plastic, and holding a carrier-bag of the kind used for air travel.

I think we are all struck dumb.

What are you doing here? says the woman.

I don't suppose it's any exaggeration to say that those present had some difficulty in answering that question. I think that we Icelanders even looked a little shamefaced, not unlike little boys who are caught pulling up turnips in someone else's vegetable garden. But I should make the point that the winter-pasture shepherds betrayed no emotion, whether because of the radiance of thought that constantly characterizes these peo-ple, or because astrotelekinesis, cosmobiology and bioradio-therapy are typically commonplace in their eyes and require no explanation.

But when replies were a little slow in coming from those present, the woman did not wait but walked straight to the door of the house. The sheriff's seal on a piece of string barred the way. The woman did not even have to produce her scissors; she brushed it aside with her hand like a cobweb. Then she brought out her key-ring, searched for the right key for a moment, opened the door, went in, closed the door behind her, and was gone.

Langvetningur: Who is that woman? Did she break the seal?

Jódínus: Who was she? There is only one woman who opens this house.

Langvetningur: What woman is that?

Jódínus: I'm just a workingman and right from the start I have been paid hourly rates for keeping my mouth shut. Now I don't open my mouth unless I get hourly rates for talking. As far as I'm concerned you can believe that this woman came down with the rain.

Embi: What do you mean, came down with the rain? (NB: There was no reply, but in the dictionary it says this phrase is used about earthworms that rain down from the sky.)

Langvetningur: There's a light showing between the cur-tains. She has put on the lights. So it's a human being. So it has worked!

Jódínus: Did you think she didn't know how to use electric-ity? Didn't you know what you were raising? What does the bishop say?

Embi: To my knowledge I wasn't raising anything at all. I am present here as the emissary of the Ministry of Ecclesiastical Affairs.

Jódínus: What do these bearded mysteries from the other side of the globe say?

They said nothing.

The law of determinants had been at work: cosmobiology and epagogics had proved themselves, "bioinduction" had taken place, as the American puts it, using a word I have in fact been unable to find in seventeen English dictionaries but that could be everyday argot among holy men and mystic supermen in California. But such people were presumably long past giving a shout if they raise something from the dead, indeed the burning-eyed sleeper Epimenides needed to do nothing but look with those eyes of his, and a marvel occurred.

The well-rounded woman stands bareheaded at her doorway, her face in shadow while the light streams out through the open door behind her. On second thought, the woman has doubtless thought it right to ascertain who these men were to whom she had absentmindedly bidden good evening as she was entering her house earlier.

Woman: Do you live here, my lads?

Langvetningur, with a big horse in his spectacles, but all the same like a little boy: We each come from different corners of the earth on account of a trifling matter. This man here is from the Andes, and the other, I understand, is from somewhere in the realm of Alexander the Great. But that one over there is a spiritual man from California.

Woman: And you yourself, my dear?

Langvetningur: Well, I'm really from so far away that no one knows any longer where my district lies and I hardly know it myself. My name is Helgi Jónsson from Torfhvalastaðir in Langvatnsdalur. I'm the man who was always looking for big horses. One day I bumped into the Master. He says to me: I shall teach you cosmobiology. At first I thought I had never heard such nonsense. I am what they call a teacher-training college man, and therefore I believe in common sense. Human-breed improvers from the galaxies, that's simply not for horse traders. That's another foal from a different mare, as they say. But what happened? Doesn't the horse one least dares to believe in always prove to be the best? From that day onwards I could not think of anything else. I am like the man in the Bible who heard about a good mare, sold all his possessions, and set off and bought her. Finally I published the Master's book at my own expense. I haven't in fact got my money back yet, but he shall always have his reward in Christian conscience who has put the truth into print even though no one wants to read it. How do you do and be welcome, madam, I am pleased to meet you.

Jódínus: If you don't mind, I'm just an ordinary working-man and my name is Jódínus, but all the same I'm the one who represented the Tycoon here, responsible for all his doings. But my name is also Álfberg and I am a poet, though I'm not a modern poet and I don't fancy these newfangled poets who can't alliterate properly. It was I who transported the materials for all the quick-freezing plants hereabouts; it's not my fault if they are all either subsidised or bankrupt or never even got started. Perhaps there will be a local subsidy of a million tomorrow. I also transported the palisander here for the Tycoon's house; it is the only building at Glacier that makes a profit. I seem to remember, by the way, that we are related, my good woman, so you must excuse me for being informal with you.

That milk drinker over there with the electrical apparatus for spies, he claims to be a bishop, but I'm not afraid of fellows like that. Tell the woman what your name is!

The undersigned didn't consider himself a turnip thief in this vegetable garden and saw no reason to give an account of himself. Indeed the woman took no notice of me and ignored Jódínus's introduction. She turned towards the foreigners and spoke to them with severity tempered with compassion, the same tone that housewives have always used for giving orders to winter-pasture shepherds both in the sagas and in Jón Árnason's folktales: James the butler is waiting for you in the capital, so try to get on your way at once. He has plane tickets for you tomorrow night.

Jódínus: I am driving south to my home in the twelve-tonner, and it's no trouble to give a lift to a few World Redeemers and take them part of the way.

Saknússemm the Second pulled out a handful of American dollar bills from underneath his blanket and waved them.

Woman: Where did you get that money, *vous pauvres diables vous?*

Saknússemm II: Lord Maitreya who created us from nothing and has now popped home to the fifth heaven—he has also created money for us to live on until he comes back after three thousand years.

Lute-player, now stopped squeezing geophysical drops from his strings: I have his head in my bag.

The sleeper Epimenides got to his feet, turned a half-circle, smiled out to sea, and was ready to leave.

Woman: Yes, try and get back to Los Angeles quickly, my poor wretches; you can catch cold here.

In explanation and excuse the woman addresses this remark

to us: "He" never tired of collecting such poor wretches, and never wearied of dragging them along behind him to and fro across the world.

When the woman had briskly settled the question of the winter-pasture shepherds, as described, she turned to the matter that was truly timely and pointed to the zinc box on the veranda in front of the door.

What was in that container?

I suppose it was really a psychological phenomenon in itself that everyone should have forgotten about the box, including the undersigned, who after all had been briefed at great length by the spiritual authorities to find out what was in it. At last, in public view, a marvel had occurred of the kind that people never tire of mocking, because marvels pertain to theology. But this time it so happens that the only thing lacking is an attestation from a notary public for the marvel to become scientific; unfortunately it was overlooked at the time to have an attestation from such a person to accompany the Easter message of the New Testament. But what happens when attestable people see a miracle occur and a woman resurrect? It's like offering a whole cake to a dog. People became downright impotent. Most people look at their watches, have other things to attend to, have to hurry away. When the woman reminded them, however, they pulled themselves together enough to start prising up the lid of the box.

It was no more than a month to the solstice, night in the northwest would soon become morning in the southeast, yet the electric light coming through the door behind the woman did not affect the natural light. When the lid was removed, this light glistened on the contents of the box. The light shone dazzlingly on the material that filled the box to the brim, and glit-

tered like a terrible jewel, larger than if all the principal dia-
monds in the world were put together. It was a frozen block.
The ice had certainly started to thaw considerably, as was said
before, after many hours of transportation in the above-zero
temperatures of the lowlands, and had started to come away
from the rims of the container. They turned the box upside
down so that the contents came free. Now one could see through
the melting ice, and it was clear that this long, gleaming, and
translucent block housed a most beautiful salmon. A fish of
this size has been lost by all great anglers, and they never forget
it afterwards. When the winter-pasture shepherds had over-
turned this moist ice-block at the woman's feet, they threw the
packing out onto the paving and the Icelanders collected the
debris. Helgi of Torfhvalastaðir took the wood for later use,
while the poet Jódínus secured the zinc.

And as the salmon lies radiating the colours of the rainbow
at the woman's feet, imprisoned in its diamond, the three winter-
pasture shepherds make ready to leave. They gird themselves in
their poncho-blankets. The lute-player puts under his arm
the lute, which preserves in its strings a geophysical drop, and
pretends he has stolen the head of Professor Doctor Godman
Sýngmann and is going to shrink it.

The sleeper Epimenides, with his white eyes, his blue beard
and hair, and the smile from the shadow of the eternal mango
tree—he knocks his forehead thrice on the floor in front of the
woman and lays the scurvy grass and crowberry heather from
his garland at her feet, then gets up effortlessly like a man made
of rubber and glides down the veranda steps and now has no
flowers left in his garland. When he reaches the bottom of the
steps he turns round and kisses the bare earth in front of the
woman.

Saknússemm II, who will perhaps be burned one day for disputatious writings and alchemy like our compatriot Saknússemm the First, whom the French reckon the King of Denmark burned—he is the only one of the winter-pasture shepherds to address any words to the woman: Would you give me a receipt, madam?

Woman: A receipt? For what?

Saknússemm II: You have been resurrected. We are obliged to produce a receipt for everything we do. Perhaps the museum will lay claim to you.

Woman: What are you talking about, my poor wretch?

Saknússemm II: The epagogic museum that Lord Maitreya founded in California.

Woman: Ah, the flies' house! *Comprendo*. What poor dear wretches. Perhaps I'll be nice and give you a receipt for that fish all the same, even though I never ordered fish.

Saknússemm II: All right.

The woman tears a page from her notebook and scrawls on it these words in English, "Received one fish," and puts some name underneath, "sister Helena" or something like that, it seemed to me.

Saknússemm II looks closely at the slip of paper and finally tucks it away: All right then. Our mission is concluded. Eat your fish now, madam. Thank you. Good night.

38

The Woman Guðrún Sæmundsdóttir from Neðratraðkot

The woman from her doorway: What am I to do with the fish?

Embi, alone on the veranda when the other visitors had gone: I don't know, madam. You have given a receipt for it.

Woman: What are you doing here?

Embi: I hardly know either. I beg your pardon for being here.

Woman: Were you in tow with these poor wretches?

Embi: Oh no, I wouldn't say I was with them. Could I have a few words with you even though it's rather late?

Woman: What did you say you were, again?

Embi: I represent the bishop.

Woman: Yes, of course, that's right. Do come in, please. I'll shut the door; it's a little chilly. Do have a seat. You seem to be a nice young man. I think that though you're not a bishop yet you will be one someday. It must be fun.

While the woman was talking to me she was finding her way about the house, opening this door and that, peering into shelves and cupboards: And here's a kitchen with an electric cooker and everything, she said aloud to herself. Won't take long to make some coffee. I think I've got a tin of it out in the Imperial.

Embi: Thanks, but I've given up coffee for the rest of my life.

Woman: There must be a status symbol like whisky somewhere around. I don't drink myself, as a matter of fact.

Embi: Nor do I.

Woman: You are certainly going to be a bishop one day.

The woman had now twice made me a bishop in a relatively short time, and there was really nothing more to be done for a while. She opened the curtains and looked silently out at the churchyard: That fresh grave, is that his?

Embi: Dr. Godman Sýngmann was buried there two days ago.

Woman: Were you at the funeral?

Embi: On the bishop's behalf, yes.

Woman: Did it go well?

Embi: It was all right.

The woman looked out of the window. Judging by a certain light on her cheek and hair, and the fresh sound of the terns' cries outside, I felt it to be morning somehow.

She had her hair up in a Grecian knot, like Venus de Milo— it's called a washerwoman bun here in Iceland. I had not thought the woman big at first on the veranda, but now I could see that she was rather big. When she had gazed her fill at the grave she took her knitting needles from the carrier-bag and yawned silently so that one could see down her throat, like a lion, before she started knitting. She sat down with her ball of wool beside her on the twin settee where Dr. Sýngmann had given up the ghost. This woman seemed to live without any effort, yet none can tell what comes naturally and what through discipline in such a woman.

She explained as if it were of no importance that she had not heard of "this" until in Paris the day before yesterday, the day of the funeral. Of course James cabled everyone except me, she said, and went on: I was never popular with butlers in that blessed household. I got a telegram from old Mowitz and the rest in London. Some come late, but come nonetheless.

That apart, the undersigned refers to the comments by local people about these women, particularly to what Tumi Jónsen the parish clerk declared here in this report, chapters 8–11 (concerning women who do not sleep, etc.); and also remarks by pastor J. Prímus along the same lines. And though the woman yawned once as she took up her knitting it doesn't refute the fact that long journeys by day and night have little effect on such women. I felt the woman grow larger on the sofa as she sat there knitting, having given a receipt for the fish. She was perhaps almost 180 cm tall. Of her other measurements I cannot speak. *Vollschlank* was sometimes used of women one cannot describe except in German; it means not fat, much less thin. She was certainly broad in the shoulder, and the "dowager's hump" had perhaps begun to protrude a little; but the neck is still so youthful that there is no dewlap under the chin. On the other hand, such women quickly become bosomy if they don't go in for sport; doesn't have to stem from indolence. She was wearing a coat of light-blue velvet, very loose-fitting (such as younger women sometimes wear when they are expecting), which reached down to the hem of a beige dress; she was wearing pale suede boots. This woman wore no jewellery of any kind.

The undersigned produced his report to see where matters stood, then chose a special opening under the heading of

Unexpected Conversations, which might well prove to be outside the official brief from the Ministry of Ecclesiastical Affairs.

Embi: It so happens that the bishop has sent me here to this parish to make some inquiries about a trifling matter. There is something I would like to ask you about. But I would point out that you do not need to answer me at all if you don't wish to, and you can be as evasive as you like; nor do you have to tell the truth in reply to my questions, and you may use *reservatio mentis* as much as you like, though I hope you do not know what that is. It is our task in the south to find the truth.

Woman: I have never concealed anything that mattered. On the other hand I am not a stranger to the Jesuits. Question away as you please, my dear.

Embi: What is your name, if I may ask?

Woman: My name is Guðrún Sæmundsdóttir from Neðra-traðkot, and I am the daughter of the couple there.

Embi: Well I must say you rather took me aback there, madam. But there's nothing to be done about that. One asks and asks and always the answers become more incomprehensible than the question. In the end one becomes an idiot.

Woman: Go ahead, my dear.

Embi: The bishop wants to hear about status.

Woman: Status, what's that?

Embi: What you are.

Woman: I am the pastor's wife here.

Embi: I didn't know there was a pastor's wife here. I thought the pastor lived alone—apart from Miss Hnallþóra.

Woman: I am his wife.

Embi: But been away rather a long time, isn't that so?

Woman: Thirty-five years. That's not a very long moment of time.

Embi: When you signed the receipt for the fish just now, it looked as if you wrote some strange name or other.

Woman: Sometimes before I know it I write that name when I take delivery of fish. I was once in a Spanish convent and took delivery of fish at the gate and was called Elena.

Embi: I see, so you were a nun.

Woman: It so happened that I had been in charge of a bordello in Buenos Aires for a few years. But I have always found pleasures boring, so I entered a convent. About the time I had finished *el noviciado* and was to take the veil, my father-confessor, who was impotent, discovered that I couldn't be a virgin. You see, I had forgotten to mention that I was a married woman and a pastor's wife up north in Iceland.

Embi: I don't suppose you knew a girl called Úa?

God help you, my boy, said the woman. Who put that into your head?

But as I sit there engrossed in my papers and at a loss for an answer, all of a sudden a woman I did not recognise started laughing. When I looked up the laughter had stopped.

Who was that laughing? I asked.

Woman: When I had gone out into life, before I knew it I started to be called Úa.

In fact there was nothing in this woman's demeanour that aroused sensuality. Without doubt she was like any other age-ing woman if one began to think about "life," and indeed it was not until she had drawn attention to it herself that I remembered that everyone is part of the enigma of time.

Embi: "Úa"—what does that mean?

Woman: It is easily understood in France. Also in Buenos Aires. On the other hand, I have heard that the name is bad in Denmark. It is pronounced with the stress on the *ú*; then a short *a. Ooh-a.* Some people never learn to pronounce it nor to decline it. In the United States they think it is a South Sea Islands language. One man in Los Angeles offered a thousand dollars for it for his daughter who had still not been conceived—and got it. Yes—that girl, she is now dead. It is a word from the language of the eiderducks at home, úa-úa; they taught me to understand life.

Embi: I gather from various things you say that you are the woman who three years ago was said to have died abroad?

Woman: Yes, I died that year, the year I lost my Úa.

Embi: So you have lost children, madam? Accidents?

Woman: We do not know that, my young friend. Are there ever accidents where God is concerned?

Embi: Doesn't it take quite a lot to be able to ask such a question in all seriousness, madam?

That is true, said the woman. Thank God that accidents happen. Then one first gets to know God. No, my children didn't die. It was only I who died and moved into another house—the other house.

The woman looked up and laughed another woman's shrill, automatic laughter.

Embi: You laugh?

Woman: The woman in the other house laughs.

Embi: Perhaps we'll turn to something else with your permission, madam. Hmm. What do you say about the notion that your soul was conjured into a fish three years ago and preserved up on the glacier until this evening?

The woman stopped knitting and answered in amazement: God bless you and keep you, you poor man.

Embi: Thank you. But I don't know if there is any point in noting that reply.

The woman went on looking at me for a while and was obviously nonplussed. She said: Aren't you just a tiny bit limited, my little one?

Embi: It is only asses who are ever employed to make official reports. If I weren't one, no one would have asked me to do this kind of thing. I hope you forgive me.

Comprendo, said the woman.

I looked out of the door and saw that the ice was nearly melted from the fish and there was a pool on the veranda. As a matter of fact, I was surprised that the woman hadn't been still more astonished. It was obvious that this woman was very experienced and that it wasn't easy to surprise her with anything, least of all with metaphysics. I made for safer ground and asked casually: What are you going to do with this fish?

Woman: Come and have some salmon tomorrow.

And then the woman from the other house laughed unnaturally heartily for a little.

Guðrún Sæmundsdóttir put on her spectacles because she had dropped a stitch. She picked up the stitch and continued the row she was on.

There is a strange restfulness in being close to a woman who is knitting. Could it be because by knitting, women succeed in suppressing their own inner tensions? At first I had thought it was a pullover but now it looked as if it had a thumb.

Embi: So you knit mittens, madam?

Woman: Yes, I knit sea-mittens.

Embi: Why?

Woman: How very immature you are, my dear. Why do I knit sea-mittens, what a question! Because I am a knitter, of course—what do you think, my love?

Embi: I am wondering for whom you are knitting sea-mittens.

Woman: I have introduced sea-mittens to Peru.

Embi: To Peru, I see. You are the first Icelander in my life I have heard pronouncing the word Peru correctly—with the stress on the second syllable. It would be fun to hear a little bit about the country you pronounce so well, and which deserves sea-mittens.

Woman: Yes, although you know everything, you young men, you perhaps don't know that Peru is the biggest fishing nation in the world.

Embi: The Icelanders are peripheral people and never see what is central in anything.

Woman: In Peru there are a thousand times more seamen than in Iceland. But they had never seen sea-mittens before I arrived. Since then I always send between a hundred and a hundred and fifty pairs of sea-mittens to Lima every year.

Embi: Is there always a market for sea-mittens out there in the south?

Woman: They are mostly used as gifts for tombolas. The remainder is stolen in Paris. But I have also crocheted and knitted many a mantilla for dark-eyed girls to put on when they go to church to kiss the Redeemer and to take off when they meet a man.

Embi: Isn't it rather a depressing job to knit sea-mittens that are stolen in Paris before they reach the tombola in Lima?

Woman: Oh, it's so sweet talking to you, my love. It really wakes me up. And that's because you talk so ironically. Almost like a Frenchman. I have never known how to talk ironically.

Embi: If I am to tell you what I think, I think that people don't start knitting sea-mittens except from boredom, and great boredom at that.

Woman: Work is God's glory, my grandmother used to say.

Sea-mittens or mantillas, does it make any difference? I have always been ready to give my last penny to be allowed to work.

Embi: There are some who say that it is only the rich who can afford to be poor.

Woman: Nothing is boring except having fun.

Embi: You no doubt have some social system or other ready to hand, where people pay to be allowed to knit sea-mittens but get paid by the hour for going to dances and the cinema, or out riding?

Woman: Social system? What's that again?

Embi: The State—

Woman: Ah, the State; *comprendo*. You mean the club?

Embi: Not necessarily the club, much rather the offices; and then all those who are dependent on the offices.

Woman: The offices, ah yes, now I know what you mean. Sure, sure, I know them all right. That's where people sit in a waiting room with their little concerns and a little image of the Redeemer on a cord round their necks in the belief that there is someone in the innermost office. No, that wasn't what I meant, and I have nothing ready to hand to put in its place.

Embi: Are you also an anarchist, madam?

Woman: Oh no, I don't think so. We only knew my poor dead Albenes and those fellows. Mundi sometimes sold them patents for the navy. They made people believe there was some-one in the innermost office. So the people waited all day and gave their Redeemer a little kiss every now and again in gratitude for the authorities being so obliging and *muy bien*, and were told to come back tomorrow. But Albenes and the others were just up in the mountains at the time, shooting peasants for fun like all great men; or else they were lying around in the brothels.

Embi: Is that not a little exaggerated, madam? I'm in considerable doubt whether I ought to put this on record.

Woman: Oh, I think I know what I'm talking about, I who was in charge of one of these *casas* of theirs for years. We sometimes got such *casas* from the navy as payment for the patents. It's better to knit sea-mittens.

39

An Account of
G. Sýngmannsdóttir

This has become rather complicated. It keeps adding to itself, however small the questions. It will be a big task to edit this and get it into shape as a report. The woman leads me round in circles, and no doubt there are many still to come. Perhaps there will be no end to it, and morning on the way.

Embi: Can you remember where we started?

Woman: Did we start on something, my sweet? I didn't notice.

Embi: There is really only the one matter that troubles the bishop concerning you. The rest is incidental.

Woman: Yes, I have known many bishops. Some of them were very nice people. But the eminent sometimes think that life is simpler than it really is.

Embi: First I noted that you are the pastor's wife at Glacier.

But then all at once you are in charge of a bordello in Buenos Aires. In the same breath become a nun in South America, Saint Helena. And lost children in accidents in North America. Now a knitter—did you say sea-mittens, isn't that pushing it a bit far, madam? And your name is Guðrún Sæmundsdóttir from Neðratraðkot! Let's hope the name is entered in the parish registers. But first of all I want to ask: does such a woman not have responsibilities and duties?

Woman: Such as?

Embi: Well, for instance, why did the pastor's wife not remain with the pastor?

Woman: I think bishops would probably find most other things easier to understand than that.

Embi: May I call your attention to the fact that we are Lutheran here.

Woman: I am a Catholic.

Embi: Orthodox?

Woman: Yes, orthodox.

Embi: Have you not been excommunicated?

Woman: I entered into Christian marriage and have never been divorced. I have always had my husband whom I have loved and respected and no other man.

Embi: What about the American who had children with you?

Woman: Americans are children. Children believe in guns and gunmen. One hundred forty-seven gunshots in children's television a week. In children's films there have to be child murders. Have you noticed that if you cut the Cross diagonally in two at the middle, you have two guns, one for each hand? They are adorable children.

Embi: Why did you not remain with your husband whom you loved and respected? You weren't abducted?

Women: Oh, no no.

Embi: Were you stolen, madam?

Woman: I was bought.

Embi: Was it Godman Sýngmann?

Woman: He put the money on the table, yes.

Embi: Is it possible to buy people?

Woman: It is possible to ask a shepherd girl to go riding even though she is married to a pastor. It is possible to ask her to go riding round the whole world. But when she comes back after a generation, she has been there all the time.

Embi: Isn't it correct to say Professor Godman Sýngmann was a polygamist?

Woman: Who says so?

Embi: The butler cabled four widows.

Woman: Yes, and I've now taken the Imperial off him. We'll see to it that he steals no more. Were it not for me, the poor wretch would be in jail where he belongs. I am going to save him from jail on this occasion, too.

Embi: Have you anything else to say about the wives of Godman Sýngmann? No exaggeration in that story?

Woman: Let us hope he had many. He was a man of the world. He lived all over the world. His friends the Imams had as many as three hundred wives. Both in Benares and Los Angeles they called him Lord Maitreya. What is a man like that to do with one female creature or two? Buddha had ten thousand women in his belly. When Mundi came back to Iceland as a young engineer and inventor with his millions from Sumatra and Australia, some people thought his hair so very soft. A shepherd girl from Neðratraðkot, newly married to a penniless country pastor and scarcely even started to sleep with him— she got the world as a gift from Mundi.

Embi: Who are these women? And where can they be found?

Woman: Doesn't interest me. It's three years now since I sent him a telegram to regard me as dead. I don't know about others.

Embi: Did he believe that you were actually dead?

Woman: What do the gods believe? That's one of the things we'll never find out. We only know that they are above earthly life. It doesn't occur to me for a moment that there's a single trace of Mundi under that soil there in the churchyard.

Embi: That's my business, madam: I am the one who was responsible to the ecclesiastical authorities for this funeral. On the other hand I suppose the ministry will want to know where you yourself stand as regards the law of the land and as regards international matrimonial law also, as regards the professor's other wives, if there are any.

Woman: What laws are you talking about, my dear boy?

Embi: For example, laws against polygamy.

Woman: How should laws about polygamy concern me?

Embi: Excuse me for saying so, and mercifully there are no witnesses present: but I understood that you were married to two men at once and one of them was married to several women at the same time as you. Is that correct?

The woman stopped knitting: Who says that? What extraordinary rubbish to hear from such an intelligent boy!

Embi: I'm not accusing anyone, far from it. Least of all you. I was just sent here like any other ass to make inquiries about things that don't concern me at all and that I don't care about at all. As I said, there is no need for you to give me any answers.

Woman: I was not Godman Sýngmann's wife. I am his daughter.

Embi: You'll excuse me for choking a little on that, madam. How are my superiors to understand this?

Woman: Sýngmann was a British citizen. He adopted me under British law, according to which the one who adopts has to be twenty years older than the one adopted. I was seventeen, and Mundi was forty. I am his only child.

Embi: If I may ask, what did people in your district do when they were so amazed they couldn't speak?

Woman: They stuck five fingers up their arse.

Embi: You must forgive me for not being sufficiently grown-up to use bad words except in moderation.

Woman: I pity you a little. A lot of people have found it difficult to understand me, unfortunately, especially I myself—and it was no better when I was younger. I don't know how I can make you understand me. A romantic girl—do you know what that is?

Embi: No.

Woman: Never slept with a romantic girl?

Embi: It must be terrible.

Woman: What a very honest boy I think you must be! That's how it was nonetheless, my dear. There is nothing to hinder a girl who has become a pastor's wife for romantic reasons from falling in love with a man of the world. But though I was naive, it never occurred to Mundi, of course, to propose marriage to me. He simply put money on the table. And when he had adopted me he sent me to a convent school in Paris, because obviously a man of that kind didn't want to have a stupid daughter. It wasn't until much later when I was in my twenties that he wanted me as his mistress for a while, as if to make his apologies. But by then we had in fact become abstracts to one another, because he was always away on other continents making money and I had been learning needlework and Christian religion and German conjugations with the nuns and become a

Catholic. And romance gone by the board, and long out of fashion in Paris. But I continued to be his daughter, of course, in spite of that.

Embi: I put it on record, then, that romance was gone by the board and long out of fashion in Paris. Excuse me, madam, but what is romance? I mean, how would one define romance for the Ministry of Ecclesiastical Affairs?

I'll tell you, replied the woman. When I was growing up, the greatest man in the world was Blondin. And "Parlez-moi d'Amour" was everybody's song—especially if you didn't know French. It took me unawares when I came to Paris to find that everyone had long ago forgotten my Blondin, and those who sang aloud about *l'Amour* were thought to be mad. Now they sang "Parlez-moi de la Pédérastie."

Embi: Who was Blondin?

Woman: There you are, *mon petit*! Knows everything and hasn't even heard of Blondin! Oh, they stretched a rope across Niagara Falls and made the poor wretch dance on it. That's what's done nowadays with those luckless creatures who are put into canisters and sent whirling round the earth—or was it perhaps round the moon. Human beings are constantly inventing new ways of maltreating one another. *C'est la vie.*

Embi: And what happened to that ugly new song you mentioned?

Woman: That was just about the only thing that some rosy-cheeked blue-eyed girls from Scandinavia learned during their first winter in Paris in those days. Now everyone has long since forgotten that too, apart from a few wretches like poor Saint Genet, whom they now want to turn into the principal saint and national poet of France. On the other hand Mundi was never the same person after having taken me from his best friend back home in Iceland. To atone for that, it wasn't long before he made his daughter his sole heir in an indissoluble will, which is deposited with old Mowitz and his confrères in London. That's to say I own all these possessions of Mundi's all over the world, wherever they happen to be. If your bishop is short of a plug of tobacco, my dear, just tip me the wink.

Embi: Are you going to use this money yourself, madam? And what for, if I may ask?

Woman: Well it goes without saying that the legacy comes into the household here, pastor Jón's and mine. My husband will of course decide what is to be done with this money. I pay no attention to matters of finance. I live by my knitting needles.

Embi: Would you let me write a book about you sometime, madam? About your relationship with Dr. Godman Sýngmann? And preferably another book about him, in fact?

Woman: Go ahead. Write as many books as you like, my dear.

Embi: He was a very remarkable man.

Woman: He was a wonderful man. No one who got to know him was ever the same again. He was the greatest man on earth next to my husband, pastor Jón Prímus. But he didn't have communion.

Embi: Eh? Did I hear you wrong again, madam? Did Professor Dr. Godman Sýngmann not have communion?

Woman, for the second time: The dear man, this wonderful man, can you imagine it: he did not have communion.

Embi: I thought he not only had communion, but had The Supercommunion itself, written with capital letters.

Woman, for the third time: He did not have communion.

Embi: And I thought he had even had communion with higher sentient beings in distant solar nebulae!

Woman: Am I not telling you that he lacked communion?

Embi: Do you perhaps mean communion with earthly beings such as I hope you are? That he had for instance to suffer the kind of spiritual and physical break that makes marriage meaningless?

Woman: He lacked the communion that says: Thou shalt love the Lord thy God with all thy heart, all thy soul, and all thy body, and thy neighbour as thyself.

Embi: But now that they have discovered that man hates himself more than any other living creature, how is he then to go about loving other men? Kill them perhaps?

Woman: *Qu'est-ce que tu as, mon petit!* What's the matter with you, little one?

Embi: Do you have communion, madam?

Woman: How old are you?

Embi: Twenty-five.

Woman: I am fifty-two. Twenty-five and fifty-two: it's the same age difference as there was between San Juan de la Cruz and Saint Theresa when they met for the first time.

Embi: And what happened?

The woman stopped knitting; she stood up: Go to bed, little one.

She opened the curtains in the dawn, and the gleam on the too-green homefield was almost uncomfortable.

The undersigned apologized for having forgotten himself, stuffed into his pocket the notebook that contained the main points, and switched off the slow-running tape recorder. The woman opened the door and let me out.

Embi: The ice has almost melted from your fish, madam. The water is flooding the porch. If we don't meet again, I thank you for your ready answers and the pleasure of meeting you. I'm off to do my packing once again. My bus goes at a quarter to twelve.

Woman: Have you forgotten that you are invited to have some fish tomorrow?

40

Reality as the Head-Bone of a Fish

It took the undersigned some time to pack his things into the duffel bag yet again, and especially to scribble out a summary of the day's events from memory. The shadows thrown on the ground by a low house, even by the wall of a vegetable garden, were so huge that they were completely unreal. But what drew me to the window was the unusual vehemence of the birds outside, violent aggression accompanied by screams that bore no relation to the neutral night-bleating such as I had become accustomed to hearing from the cliffs through my sleep. If one looked out during the night at this time of year one would see one or two birds at the most, gliding past on some inscrutable errand. By complete contrast, there were now countless myriads of birds eddying and screaming over the farmhouse and the homefield. There were not just kittiwakes there, the inhabitants of the cliff; fulmars and greater black-backed gulls from the fishing banks, herring gulls, and even great skuas had come to take part in this choir; as far as I could see, some of them were clawing at one another upside down in the air. The churchyard overflowed with these hell-birds; they were crowded on the church roof and the bungalow. As a reporter from the Ministry of Ecclesiastical Affairs I had no other choice than to stare passively at this phenomenon of Nature; besides, I would have had no authority to shoot even if I had had a field-gun.

This fiendish uproar was at its height for about fifteen minutes, and then subsided. The churchyard, however, continued to be covered with birds; except that now they sat still as if they were holding a meeting over some matter of importance that had taken place, and only screeched one at a time. More and more of them took off and flew away in silence to the sea. Others peered all around as if they were waiting for another miracle. Why is it that birds look far bigger on the ground than in flight? They looked of supernatural size to me. At last my interest in natural history was exhausted and I left these birds to themselves on the graves of the dead in the dawn, and went to sleep. Should I not delete everything on these pages about birds and fish? But there's a risk that there would be little left if birds and fish are not to count.

Now all my things were in the duffel bag and there was nothing left but to say good-bye to pastor Jón Prímus and congratulate him on the fact that his wife had come home and everything was nice and settled at Glacier and also, let's hope, at the Ministry of Ecclesiastical Affairs.

I knocked on various doors and doorposts in the farmhouse but there was no reply. The fairy-ram woman, the one with the second sight, had perhaps got wind that the pastor's wife was coming. Perhaps she calculated that now that she had served coffee to the Great Powers, and with the archenemy close by, it was

time for housekeepers for their part to go out into the world and
have fun, like pastors' wives. Whatever the cause, no matter how
much the undersigned tapped on doors, there was no sign of life.

The pastor would often return from his mending expedi-
tions sometime between dawn and midmorning, but sometimes not at all; it was usually difficult to see any trace of
whether he had been home or not. This time on the whole
there were no signs of whether anyone had been coming or
going, nor on the whole that there had been any life at all for a
long time in this parsonage. The twelve-tonner was gone from
the paving; the buttercups were awake between the paving
stones, those that hadn't been crushed beneath those eighteen
wheels. The Langvetningur of the big horses was lost in the
fogs of far-off districts that perhaps are not of this earth—
that parish officer, cosmologist, and horse trader who single-
handedly had refuted Goethe's saying that all theory is grey.

Although people in the ministry might not be inquiring specially about calves, the undersigned reckons that the farm-calf
here deserves good marks for conduct and progress. Higher
powers have released him from his tether, and some rams have
come to visit him. The grass he is now guzzling was only in
God's mind ten days ago.

Last night it was asserted that Godman Sýngmann's head had
been stolen. It was also firmly alleged last night that the professor's fresh grave in the churchyard was not genuine. What does
Tumi Jónsen say, that historian of historians at Glacier? Would
he declare upon his Christian conscience that reliable men reckoned that a notable angler, whom some sources nevertheless state
to have been a tycoon, was buried in this churchyard? Is there
anything more likely than that honest and truthful men of the
historian's progeny will come forth and maintain, not without

good cause, that this churchyard had been abandoned for fifty years and that some practical joker had amused himself by using a grave there and putting something or perhaps nothing into it? Perhaps there were some coarse youngsters from other districts at work, or some naughty children, to hoax people. It could well be right, as some people think, that this Godman Sýngmann was some other person altogether.

I was beginning to fear I would be bringing my superiors down south nothing but a book of dreams instead of a report from this mission to Glacier. It would make matters worse if one had to add a book of dream interpretations.

I tiptoed to the veranda of the bungalow to see if I could find any signs of something having happened. I saw none at first glance and became afraid. There is no more terrifying experience for a Christian than to discover he has suddenly become a rationalist. The curtains were drawn at the windows just as the butler James Smith had left them, no sign of any human habitation anywhere around, the house dead. Where was the great salmon? Vanished, as if the earth had swallowed it! Merely a little more bird dirt than before on the veranda. But when I began to inspect the place more closely, I noticed the county seal lying in a corner. The seal, in other words, had been broken, and scarcely in a dream. But who had broken it? Was it this woman? Or some other woman? Or some practical jokers? What would Tumi Jónsen say about it?

When I was sidling off the veranda again I caught sight of a little something that in itself was hardly worth mentioning: one head-bone of a fish, picked clean, lying in front of the woman's door. Although the woman I had dreamt was perhaps not real, there had nonetheless, whatever anyone says, been a real fish lying on the veranda last night.

41

Repairing the Quick-Freezing Plants

Truth to tell I was relieved when I got out of sight of the house, because I felt it was staring after me; yet I know perfectly well that nothing is more ridiculous than being afraid of the dark in clear weather one early morning a month before the solstice. I was hoping that pastor Jón Prímus would be in his shed repairing broken-pointed knives and worn-out sewing machines from the nineteenth century.

When I reached the gravel patch behind the lava hillock in the homefield I caught sight of the Imperial, which, for its part, had rematerialised. The car had been neatly parked, and some women's things lay on the backseat. The parish pastor's repair shed, on the other hand, was fastened with a padlock.

Pastor Jón Prímus sat on a stone by the roadside ready to leave, that's to say he had turned up the collar of his jacket and had his toolbox on his knees. Apart from that he was bareheaded and blue in the face, probably had neither slept nor eaten. He was waiting.

Good morning, pastor Jón.

Good morning.

Embi: So the big car's back.

Pastor Jón had no comment to make on that.

Embi: Are you setting off on a journey, pastor Jón?

Pastor Jón: I am waiting for a man who's giving me a lift.

Embi: Going far?

Pastor Jón: Over the mountain. The quick-freezing plant that is both out of order and bankrupt has now been given a subsidy of a million. They're going to try to start it up again. They asked me to help to repair the machinery. Jódínus is coming to fetch me.

Embi: Hmm, you know of course that Guðrún Sæmundsdóttir has arrived?

Pastor Jón: Oh, did she say that was her name?

Embi: Haven't you met her?

Pastor Jón: I saw a woman arriving late last night.

Embi: Do you really need to go away today? I have an idea the woman has come to see you.

Pastor Jón: By the way, have you had anything this morning?

Embi: Not very much, no. But it doesn't matter. I'm going south today.

Pastor Jón now got up from the stone and said: It's no good walking about like this with your mouth watering all day. I haven't had anything either, actually. But I've got some shark meat here. May I not offer you some?

Embi: I'm rather unaccustomed to shark meat. I've heard that it stinks.

Pastor Jón: Shark meat is the greatest delicacy in Iceland.

Shark meat only smells high for the first twelve years. This stuff is thirteen years old and the ammonia has long since left it. It is fragrant.

Pastor Jón pulled out of his pocket a handsome piece of this national delicacy wrapped in a newspaper and tied with pack-thread. It was a piece with an eye in it. This sea creature is called in Latin "sleepy small-head," and if one sees its eye one understands the name (*somniosus microcephalus*). The parish pastor took out his clasp-knife and cut himself a slice, chewed and smacked his lips, and pursed his mouth while he was assessing the taste, and then said: It's just right.

And in this comment there emerged the only tendency towards orthodoxy that the undersigned has been able to detect in pastor Jón Prímus.

I thought it best to be kind to the pastor, and started chewing the stuff and rolling it round my mouth out of curiosity, and found it a little strange in taste but not exactly bad. We both chewed away busily. When I had swallowed one piece, I wanted another. This is alkaline, said pastor Jón, and I can't vouch for the parish pastor's chemistry. But if only for the way he preached shark meat, everyone could see that this pastor Jón was a good pastor.

When we had chewed shark meat for a while, I came back to the matter at hand.

Embi: As was said, your wife has arrived, pastor Jón. There shouldn't be any more flies in the ointment now.

Pastor Jón: Yes, she is undoubtedly an excellent woman. And you are a young man. Why don't you have her?

Embi: Your wife?

Pastor Jón: The woman who came last night, the woman you are talking about.

Embi: Úa?

Pastor Jón: The Úa who came is not the one who went away. Because in the first place Úa cannot go away, and in the second place she cannot come back. She doesn't come back because she didn't go away. Úa remained with me, as I told you when we met here in the shed for the first time. She didn't remain just outwardly but above all within myself. Who could take your mother away from you? How could your mother leave you? What's more, she is closer to you the older you become and the longer it is since she died.

Embi: Both you, pastor Jón, and the woman herself have each separately confirmed to the bishop's emissary the fact of your marriage. Though a woman leaves for thirty-five years, that doesn't alter anything. That isn't a long moment of time in Christian belief.

Pastor Jón: There is no other Úa than the one who has always lived with me and never gone from me for a single moment. She is closer to me than the flower of the field and the light of the glacier, because she is fused with my own breath. The one thing that remains is what lives deepest within yourself, even though you glide from one galaxy to another. Nothing can change that. And now let's munch our shark meat.

Embi: According to my brief, pastor Jón, and without being involved at all: personally I would suggest that you go to see this woman and leave the quick-freezing plants alone today.

Pastor Jón: The quick-freezing plants have priority: that is the agreement.

Embi: I have heard that quick-freezing plants don't make money. Who made an agreement with whom? Let the dead bury their dead, if only for a day.

Pastor Jón: All life is built upon agreement. I thought you

knew that we have to agree upon whether we are to live; otherwise there will be war. But if we make an agreement to live, then we gladly hand over our last penny to the quick-freezing plants. And then it no longer matters whether the quick-freezing plants make money and whether the machinery in them is working or at a standstill.

Embi: Well, I'm talking on behalf of a human being, my dear pastor Jón; on behalf of a soul. It is my opinion that the soul has priority over the quick-freezing plants.

Pastor Jón: I think the quick-freezing plants are closer to God than the soul, but that is really a question of agreement.

Embi: What is the point of repairing quick-freezing plants that never pay and are run by clowns at the public expense?

Pastor Jón: Do we defend the cause of earthly life because it pays?

Embi: We have to have some glimmer or other.

Pastor Jón: There are others who live off public funds than just the quick-freeing plants. Isn't everyone bust, so to speak? If everyone isn't to be wound up because of debts at once, we have to agree about something; no matter what it costs—no matter what damned nonsense it is—there has to be agreement. People have to agree for instance about the fact that money has to be somewhere—with the rich if there's no alternative, in the banks, at the very least with the State. Yet everyone knows that money is fundamentally an invention, a fiction.

Embi: I had, however, thought that the first step would be to agree that something is true and then all try to live together by it.

Pastor Jón: It is pleasant to listen to the birds chirping. But it would be anything but pleasant if the birds were always chirping the truth. Do you think the golden lining of this cloud we see up there in the ionosphere is true? But whoever isn't ready to live and die for that cloud is a man bereft of happiness.

Embi: Should there just be lyrical fantasies, then, instead of justice?

Pastor Jón: Agreement is what matters. Otherwise everyone will be killed.

Embi: Agreement about what?

Pastor Jón: It doesn't matter. For instance quick-freezing plants, no matter how bad they are. When I repair a broken lock, do you then think it's an object of value or a lock for some treasure chest? Behind the last lock I mended there was kept one dried skate and three pounds of rye-meal. I don't need to describe the enterprise that owns a lock of that kind. But if you hold that earthly life is valid on the whole, you repair such a lock with no less satisfaction than the lock for the National Bank where people think the gold is kept. If you don't like this old, rusty, simple lock that some clumsy blacksmith made for an insignificant food-chest long ago, then there is no reason for you to mend the lock in a big bank. If you only repair machinery in quick-freezing plants that pay, you are not to be envied for your role.

Embi: What you say, pastor Jón, may be good poetry, but unfortunately has little relevance to the matter I raised with you—on behalf of the ministry.

Pastor Jón: Whoever doesn't live in poetry cannot survive here on earth.

With that, pastor Jón Prímus wrapped the rest of the shark meat in the newspaper again, put it in his pocket, and held out in farewell his big, good hand, which has already been mentioned in these pages. NB: But perhaps my memory deceives me. Jódínus had arrived with the twelve-tonner to give the parish pastor a lift over the mountain range.

42

The Poetry of Saint John of the Cross and So On

The undersigned picked up the seal from the veranda, put it in his pocket, and rang the doorbell. The woman came to the door. She had fetched her things from the car during the night and was now wearing an ankle-length dressing gown. She looked bigger than yesterday. If it's possible to call a face strongly built, it could be said of this woman; but the expression was without arrogance; no affectation in her demeanour, but her responses could be unpredictable. It cannot be denied that I couldn't tear my eyes away from an individual of the breed that was thought to be exceptional flesh here at Glacier, descended from Ireland and Spain. It's these women who never sleep. Now when I saw the woman again, scantily clad under her dressing gown, she seemed to confirm the theory that women do not attain the beauty that appealed to Stone Age man in accordance with the Willendorf Venus recipe until they

are about fifty and have had their children and lost them, with
a new era before them. The bishop's emissary said good morning.

Woman: San Juan de la Cruz!

She opened the door wide and let me in and closed it. Then
she put me on the twin settee, stroked my cheek with the back
of her hand like a child, sat down beside me, and asked me my
news; and from underneath the gown emerged a pair of unex-
pectedly young legs with good calves, which didn't start thick-
ening until above the knee, everything precisely according to
the recipe of the village of Willendorf.

Embi: Forgive me for being rather early afoot. But since the
authorities expect me to concern myself with people who don't
concern me at all, I had better tell you that pastor Jón has gone.

The woman got to her feet and fetched her knitting needles
and sat down opposite me in a chair.

Where did pastor Jón go? she asked.

Embi: The pastor went to repair a quick-freezing plant.

Woman: Can't I offer you a cup of tea, by the way, Saint?

Embi: Well perhaps, thank you, I haven't had anything
except shark meat this morning.

The woman went out to the kitchen and I studied her knitting while she was away. After a while she brought me tea and
some sweet biscuits in a rectangular packet.

Embi: If I'm not mistaken, there's a flower starting on madam's
sea-mittens.

Woman: It is my dream that sea-mittens will eventually
become so beautiful that it will be possible to wear them when
going on a Christmas visit to one's aunt.

I didn't think it right to go on about sea-mittens for the time
being: better to get to the bottom of the matrimonial situation

here before I left; the woman wasn't going to explain her "dream" further, anyway, but asked: What's a quick-freezing plant?

Embi: It's an Icelandic enterprise. Clowns build them with a subsidy from the State, then they get a subsidy from the State to run them, next they get the State to pay all the debts but finally go bankrupt and get the State to shoulder the bankruptcy. If by some accident some money ever happens to come into the till, then these clowns go out and have a party. Now a million has been provided to repair one such enterprise here on the other side of the mountain, and then of course the first thing was to send for pastor Jón.

Woman: Is this thing by any chance anything like the things they used to call icehouses in the old days?

Embi: Similar idea; different generation.

Woman: Why did he go?

Embi: You know pastor Jón.

Woman: He is my husband.

Embi: I told him you had arrived.

Woman: I hope he isn't feeling annoyed with me for any reason?

Embi: I have no authority to explain anything, madam. Indeed I have been forbidden to put forward any opinions, because in that case there's a risk that the bishop and the others would be deprived of an opportunity of thinking. I think all the same that I've sort of almost caught hold of pastor Jón's tail. He is one of the few people in the world who are so rich they can afford to be poor. Perhaps madam would like to say something on her own behalf?

Woman: You should drink your tea while it's hot, my dear. I'm going to my room now to do myself up a bit, put on some stockings and so on. She produced from her pocket a pretty little book in Spanish for me to glance at while she was in her room. It was the poetry of Saint John of the Cross.

I started on the first poem and planned to let chance decide how far I got with the book; it's called "Dark Night." This poem tells how the Soul goes out at night to meet God. This dark night is even sweeter than the first gleam of dawn itself, *noche amable más que el alborada*. Thereafter the Soul unites with God in that love of loves which is the light of transformation itself, the light of lights: *O noche que juntaste / amado con amada / Amada en el Amado transformada*. Against this poem the woman had put a red mark.

When she came back in and sat down opposite me she was wearing silk stockings high above the knee under the dressing gown; these stockings she must also have fetched from the car before people were up and about. I wanted to ask if she hadn't noticed the birds when they were eating the fish, but did not feel it right: people's sleep is their own private affair. But if she was sleeping, she must have been sleeping soundly. When she saw that I had the book open at the poem "*Noche oscura*," she couldn't resist reciting it in that language which is the loveliest of all languages.

Embi: How beautiful Castilian sounds in your mouth, madam!

Woman: I also have Spanish flesh, my dear. Some say a little bit of Irish too, worse luck.

Embi: You didn't have far to go for your Catholicism.

Woman: Isn't that a beautiful poem?

Embi: Yes and no.

Woman: Can you imagine anything more beautiful?

Embi: Yes, yes, it's a fine poem, no doubt. But if I include it as an accompanying document with my report, I'm afraid the bishop wouldn't understand it. I don't think it clarifies the matter; at least, it throws no particular light on what the ministry has instructed me to investigate. Far from it.

Woman: It comes back to what I said yesterday: you are undoubtedly rather a limited young man. What do you think is really wrong with this poem?

Embi: I don't find anything wrong with it, actually; not directly. It's as if it had been composed by a woman who thinks fondly towards her lover after successful intercourse. You mentioned Saint Genet. If the poem had been written by him I would think a depraved man was writing about another depraved man.

Woman: What astonishingly wicked thoughts you can have, a nice young man like you and soon to be a bishop! Don't you realise that Juan and Theresa were top saints? Don't you understand that this is the Soul talking to God? How can it be said in any other way?

Embi: Is such poetry not some sort of mockery on the part of the saint?

Woman: *Mais qu'est-ce que tu veux, mon petit?* There is always some sort of mockery. From one mockery to another! What should saints and poets take as an example, if not this mockery! Always some new mockery or other, and mankind never the wiser. It's like conjugating irregular verbs in German, *immer gleich schön!*

Embi: Because I hope you are both a top saint and a puritan, madam, I want to ask you about a small matter before we part: when nothing is any longer right or wrong, why have we human beings come into existence, and what are we to do?

Woman: Why are you concerning yourself with that, my dear?

Embi: Is any person so lowly that he doesn't carry the universe on his back like Godman Sýngmann? If human intelligence fails, what is there for a person to lean on?

Woman: Wouldn't you rather try to take part in human folly, my dear? It's safer. But remember, you have to do it with all your heart and all your heart and with all your heart—and what was the third thing again? Yes, consider the birds of the air, I had almost forgotten that.

Embi: How did you yourself manage?

Woman: Manage what?

Embi: To keep these looks, that colouring, that shine in the hair—

Woman: Gently, gently, my love, never say too much to women of my age, and least of all about their skin and hair, because then they might start getting mixed up. As you know, we are hunted for our skins. To tell the truth, I put a tiny bit on my face before you came.

Embi: When I talk to you I know well that you could be my mother, and I have no right to demand answers from you. And yet, I know you have lived different lives, sometimes many at a time, and must have suffered disappointments and sorrows more than most people—how do you manage to stand erect?

I play blind, said the woman.

Embi: Do you mean that the one who doesn't take the game seriously won't get disappointed?

Woman: Do you know that the birds ate my fish while I was asleep?

Embi: Yes, it was a rather unsuccessful sequel to the Easter story by the bioinductors, I think; at least not an entirely felicitous execution of the idea.

Woman: I'll have to invite you to a party at home instead.

Embi: Thank you. Well, that's just about everything, I think. My bus leaves around noon.

Woman: I'll take you in the Imperial, of course.

Embi: Thank you very much, madam, but I'll take my scheduled bus. Anything else might be misunderstood. And now I'll say good-bye. Hmm. But there was one thing I wanted to ask you before leaving: I ask out of pure curiosity, let me point out; and you don't require to answer.

Woman: You're welcome.

Embi: The first time we met you told me quite casually that you ran an establishment in South America for a time. Was it of your own free will, or against it, that you became matron of such a house?

Woman: It was a fine house. It was like any other first-class nightclub that opens in the evenings and has dancing and various numbers featuring naked girls. Dinner is at half past midnight, with honest delicacies like cuttlefish à l'Espagnol, which I still miss. It's another matter that young girls find it rather monotonous in the long run to start the day by sleeping with notables of the republic, and to be woken up at night to go up on a platform and display their bare midriffs to the public.

Embi: And you didn't find it at all immoral?

Woman: On the contrary. Never a drunk to be seen. Only rather boring. More fun knitting sea-mittens.

Embi: Not unnatural at all?

Woman: Everything very natural. And extremely Catholic. The obverse side of Catholicism. Yet I never understood brothels until I started living with the nuns. Evangelicals never understand brothels, any more than they understand the Vatican.

Embi: May I put it on record that you rate immorality and convent life roughly on a par, madam?

That I don't know, said the woman. But in our society the rules about love are made either by castrated men or impotent grey-beards who lived in caves and ate moss-campion roots. Sometimes also by perverted celibates who walk around in skirts, some say wearing women's knickers underneath. Decent women would hardly have cared to have a Church Father as a table companion.

Embi: We have now heard that the popes have become nice people.

Woman: God created all souls equal, and therefore it would be unchristian to suppose that there are fewer saints among popes than cowherds. It's another matter that when I was in North America, a woman sent an inquiry to the Vatican about a trifling matter: she asked if it were lawful to sleep with a man without starting a baby; and secondly, if a baby were conceived against the law, what did the pope think should be done? The kernel of the answer was very clear once the rhetoric had been scraped off it: beget children or else go to hell.

Embi: I thought the pope talked in Latin.

Woman: I hope nonetheless that you now understand why we have both the Vatican and the brothels in Catholicism. When I had given up my psalter in South America and had started to read advertisements in North America, the only litera-ture in the world that nowadays preaches the good and believes in life and fills the reader with confidence and optimism, I became so enamoured of an advertisement for a cream to pro-duce non-smell intercourse that I hurried out to buy a tube.

Embi: I'll note that, madam.

Woman: Yes, and add that it's a great mercy for a woman who thought she had long since stopped being aware of herself, to be allowed to talk to a polite and well-brought-up young man: you would have been just right for my daughter.

43

Uncertain Balance, Etc.

I put the notebook away in my pocket and brushed the report from my face like a swarm of midges.

The woman rose from her chair. It was still the time of day when few genteel ladies are stirring. She walked over to the window and as she brushed past my chair she patted me on the cheek once again, this time with the palm of the hand, and I caught an aroma of woman. She stood at the window and looked out to sea. Her profile was heavy with melancholy with a hint of fierce decision: an uncertain balance. Such a profile evokes in my mind an association with the pungency of a cold rose thawing the hoarfrost off itself some autumn morning. Where does creation end and destruction begin? The distinction is indeterminate, like certain decimals. The wolf-fetters you find in some works of art, fashioned from cat's footfall, bird's spit, and woman's beard—they are also present in such a profile.

Woman: Don't stare like that, my dear. Say something instead.

Embi: Where are you going, madam?

Woman: Why do you ask?

Embi: You offered to drive me—where to?

Woman: To wherever you say: there's nothing better than a polite travelling companion.

Embi: Madam, if I wanted to turn around in my life and asked to be allowed to go with you to the ends of the earth, do you think it would be out of politeness?

Woman: Haven't I told you that I have come to join my husband?

Embi: Didn't I tell you that the pastor had gone to repair a quick-freezing plant?

Woman: Are you sure I'm not a ghost?

Embi: So much the better.

Woman: Ghosts have *mauvaise odeur*.

Embi: You are fragrant.

Woman: Oh my dear God, to hear the child speak! I blush! I have never been shy like this with a man. I'm sweating! How on earth is it possible to talk like that to a woman who has had daughters and seen them into the grave! I feel giddy. (At that the woman dived into the pocket of her dressing gown for a mirror and a lipstick and did herself up half in confusion, half as if to gain time. Then she put the things away.) Haven't I told you that I adhere to the Roman Catholic faith? I can never say a word to you again, now.

Embi: I don't want to talk either. It's enough for me to have found you. I follow you in silence.

Woman: And also when I am in a wheelchair?

Embi: A wheelchair makes no difference.

Woman: And also after you have slept with me for one night?

Embi: I am a puritan.

Woman: It's terrible to hear the child talk! God in heaven help you! A puritan—where did you learn that word? Have you never been in love with a girl, or what?

Embi: Not particularly.

Woman: A little?

Embi: Yes, just a little.

Woman: And what happened?

Embi: I was shy. Not all men can command the cruelty needed to enter into marriage: there are some horrible practices involved—especially towards young girls.

For a while the woman had been looking at me out of the corner of her eye as if she were secretly amused even though of course the innocent chatter of such an inexperienced man shocked her. I was prepared for most things—except that she would burst out laughing. She tried to hold herself back at first, certainly, but that only made bad worse. Soon she lost control of herself completely. The next thing I knew, she had flopped down beside me in midlaughter. I couldn't see any special reason for such excessive laughter; perhaps there never are any logical reasons for laughter. But I was all the more aware of how the woman rose and fell, swelling, on the settee beside me. Am I so funny or something? Until I realised if I was not mistaken that the woman was crying. She fell against me with the salty weight of the surf and sobbed bitterly into my shoulder. She seized hold of my knee with her long, strong hand, the white skin on the back so strangely rough in texture.

I have no doubt said more than I should, I said, because I've never been used to women, least of all a woman like you. Now I'll get up and try to get away and ask you not to hold it against me, madam.

Woman: Can't you see yourself, man! Don't you understand that you have awakened me? It is because of you that I am aware of myself again after a long sleep. You are bound to the one you have awakened. You shall follow me to the ends of the earth. Now I am going to touch you naked.

And with that touch alone the woman had taken me to her completely.

44

Away

In Chinese literature there are many references to calves, and the master Kvangtse says these words: A wise man's expression is like that of a newborn calf. In some variants of the text, this is said to be reduced to: A wise man is a newborn calf.

This was an orphan calf and no one knew what had become of the heavy-uddered cow, his mother. He got no other swill from the fairy-ram woman Hnallþóra than cakes softened in coffee, which brought on all kinds of ailments. Though you gave him a good long scratch, he didn't have the heart to low when you left him again; he just gazed after you, gloomily. It now seemed to me that this calf's forehead was neither as bulging nor hairy as before. He seemed to be feeling better in these three or four stomachs that are said to be found in any one calf. As was said before, he had now been joined by some rams and had started to live off the abundance of the land. This company now lay chewing the cud in the churchyard. The rams stood up and stalked away when I approached, but the little calf came towards me; probably thought that I would give him some coffee.

When I had given him a little farewell scratch round the jowls and snout and had walked away, at first he watched me as I went and then trotted along behind to the lych-gate—he had somehow or other got in through it even though he couldn't get out again. He uttered a little broken-voiced sound, like the bass in a children's concertina, by closing both corners of his jaws and only just opening the mouth. And on that note this report on Christianity at Glacier should come to an end, as far as I'm concerned. I hope I'm not exceeding my terms of reference as reporter, or depriving my lord bishop of the opportunity of thinking for himself, if I end this document with the hope that the much-mentioned calf will survive.

It is doubtless right that in a report one should not expound but express. One has tried to see the thing, or at least couldn't help seeing it, with this eye that some people think we have inherited from the monsters of earth history, instead of looking with the eye that dwells deepest in universal space.

An unbreakable obligation is involved in seeing and having seen. The report has not just become part of my own blood— the quick of my life has fused into one with the report. Inadvertently I had not only been an eyewitness but also the motive power of things unknown. Who will roll away the stone from the mouth of the sepulchre for us, it was once asked. Who will redeem us from a report?

After a daylong feast with all the delicacies that are to be found in the trunk of an Imperial, the woman now drew the curtain, locked her door with a key, and the house no longer existed. The undersigned stepped into this woman's heavy car. We drove away with the evening sun on the nape of our necks—home.

Away—home.

It was one of those wholly beautiful May evenings when life's happiness lies open before mortal man. On such a day the ancient Greeks used to say: No one is happy before his dying day. The glacier, the tureen-lid of the world, arches over the secrets of the earth. It gazes after me and the woman, perfectly still, in the certainty that if it moves a tiniest fraction it would crack open for the mouse to jump out.

She drove easily along the rolling gravel road, almost free of traffic in the early summer. The mountain range to one side, broad marshlands towards the sea on the other side, with gravel banks and erosion wherever it was higher and drier. Streams and rivers cascaded off the mountains and flowed under the bridges on the road and ran down through the lowlands to the sea. The sound of birdcalls from the marshes and moors drowned the muted tyre-noise of the car. The woman drove well, certainly, but cautiously, as if she were a little out of practice.

What impelled a resourceless young man with a duffel bag into such a woman's car? What was the strange web of events into which I had suddenly become interwoven?

Was this woman's embrace perhaps that shelter which is called the mother's lap, and is the only place where people live secure on earth as long as it lasts? Was not such an embrace as this woman's a little too large to enfold a travelling boy? Were not other women at Glacier more suitable, and yet doubtless with a nice embrace in their own way? Why hadn't I leaned against Miss Hnallþóra, who had seen a ram? Wouldn't I eventually have got fish—at least on the sly—instead of the lady having baked and baked until the Great Powers ate the cakes? This young man who wandered almost unpaid about the country on behalf of the bishop, couldn't he by some knack have ingratiated himself with the merry widow Fína Jónsen from Hafnarfjörður and become a partner in the good scrubbing brush that had cleaned God's House at Glacier? Wasn't it time that the widow got rid of that boring ordinary Icelander, Jódínus the poet, whom she only loved in moderation, to put it mildly? I am sure that, thanks to such an excellent scrubbing brush, she would let me live with her down in Hafnarfjörður so that I would never have to think about anything other than the herring news on the radio and the bankrupties of the quick-freezing plants, and then go out to buy an evening paper.

Had I set off with this woman because she drove a bigger, sleeker car than other women at Glacier? And because she had inherited more than most other women, so that her millions lay scattered like brushwood all over the world in dollars, pounds, piastres, and pesos, unlikely to do anyone any good except her husband pastor Jón Prímus, who nonetheless was already the richest man in the world? Did I see in a vision jet planes and yachts, palaces and hotels, the golden sands in Miami and the skis in Garmisch-Partenkirchen—not forgetting the high culture in London Paris New York Los Angeles Buenos Aires and whatever they're called, all these places in the weekly magazines? Not forgetting Lima in Peru, where the sea-mittens went.

Who am I to have fallen victim to the sorcery of stumbling on an image that Goethe had looked for and never found, eternity in female form? Had the Almighty yet again visited the person who was as totally destitute as the snow bunting on the ice, and revealed to him a mystery? The foremost women of the world all speak to me with one mouth: the Virgin Mary with the Infant on her knee; the Greek golden age with the washerwoman bun and Venus from Willendorf, vulgar and Simon-pure with her face hidden behind her hair and her buttocks bare, the bitch-goddess of mythology, the Virgin Whore of Romanticism, Ibsen's fate-woman, the Mater Dolorosa of the Gospel—but above all the good abbess, Saint Theresa from Spain, in search of a new Saint John of the Cross.

45

Home

She stopped the car and we walked alongside running water in the world and watched mallards swimming in pools under the banks. There, too, swam the ever-bowing northern phalaropes (*phalaropus hyperboreus*). We sat on a moss-grown promontory with a bird-knoll on top, and we looked at a herd of horses in a hollow; the horses had started carrying their heads high after the ordeal of winter, biting one another, kicking up their heels, squealing, wrinkling their noses, mating. Newly marked lambs were still bloody about the head, some unlicked and only just born, others not born at all. Seldom had the sun been as bright all spring as today, but towards evening a gold-coloured fog was born far out to sea.

We came to a café that was some kind of modern heaven on earth, a compound of plastic, shellac, oil paint, turpentine, and glass but suffering from a lack of the smell of food and people.

Here there was no sustenance to be had except boiled sweets. For thirst one could get carbon water, which is also out of this world, and we drank this from an unspeaking waitress. We sat side by side at a wafer-thin plastic table that stood on spindly iron legs in this shiny turpentine heaven outside existence. The woman looked from far within herself at her companion, caught his head now and again and placed it under her cheek, sighing and whispering that tonight we would go together to the end of the world; then put the head back where it belonged. But when we came out, the golden haze that a while ago had looked like a cold theatrical fire away on the horizon had reached land; a black cloud obscured the sun.

It's safer not to go off the road now, said the man who filled our petrol tank; it's not good for walking now.

We hadn't been driving long before the fog poured over us, at first dry as dust but soon becoming dank. Within a short time there was a fine drizzle, then a mizzle with a cold breeze off the sea. The woman had to speed up the wipers so that they could manage to keep the moisture off the windscreen. It got darker, and she switched on the lights. Then I noticed that the clock on the instrument panel was nearly twelve, but I wasn't entirely clear for a moment whether it was midday or midnight; nor indeed did it matter very much.

The woman made no noticeable effort to get out of this hellish fog quickly. If anything, she drove with even greater caution than before, and she kept a particularly close watch to the seaward side on the right, as if she were expecting something from that direction. Every now and again she pulled up on the road, wound down the window, and peered out into the fog. Every time she came to a crossing she got out and inspected the turning-off even though it was only an insignificant path. I asked what she was looking for, but she made no reply. Thus we groped our way slowly through the drizzle far into the night.

After many attempts at establishing her position she finally found an insignificant side road that formed a right angle with the main road to the right. It was on sandy gravel. This side road, if it could be called a road, had been so little used that it was difficult to say when it had last had a vehicle over it; one could just make out some wheel-tracks, but they could well have been several years old, because in some places sea-campion and alpine sandwort had had peace to grow on the road, and even madder. It was onto this dubious side road that the woman now steered her big car in the fog, at a time when every bird in the land was silenced.

Where are we going?

The woman smiled at me and answered gently: Where do you think, my love, except to the end of the world?

And we continued to drive along the sandy gravel and tried to make out the track, but the fog reduced the horizon to three or four metres in front of the car.

After a while the landscape changed and this so-called road began to cross meadowlands pink with withered grass. Worst of all, the ground now became extremely soggy and this big car, nearly three tons in weight, and low-slung, began to have difficulty in making headway.

The woman's companion did not feel he had the right to make suggestions in such an unrecognisable place; at the very worst the car would get stuck. And so it did. In the middle of my determination not to think nor draw conclusions in this matter, we landed in a morass and the engine cut out. When we tried to start off again, the wheels raced; the back wheels dug themselves still deeper down. The car rested on its axle. The visibility had gone so completely that the mascot on the radiator could no longer be seen. As a result, our morass had lost its boundaries. The woman laughed until she started crying and laid my head under her cheek. We'll wade home through the marsh, said the woman.

She was wearing expensive waterproof boots up to the calves, ideal for strolling in the sunshine of Nice and San Remo. Yet she was much better shod for difficult journeys than the undersigned in his shiny black chrome-tanned leather shoes with narrow toes. When we had succeeded in pushing open the front door on one side and making a little opening, the mud from the morass poured into the car. As soon as I stepped outside I sank in up to the ankles.

The woman said we should leave our things behind, except that she was bringing with her this soft red case: There is some ham in it, and tea. Your things can wait until morning!

Embi: I have nothing but a duffel bag. But I don't dare to leave it in a morass at night. The car might sink. In the duffel bag are my shorthand notes and notebooks, my tape recorder, and all the tapes with the recordings. These are nominally speaking official documents, and if they sink or fall into the hands of dishonest people then I have broken confidence and lost my honour.

The outcome was that we fetched out my duffel bag and the woman's case, and then she locked the trunk. We set off, each carrying our own luggage. She said she could find where she lived by the smell—from here one went by the stink of decaying seaweed, which smelled like train oil.

Now we waded back and forth across this rotting swamp, I don't know for how much of the night, because the sense of time is said to be the first of the senses that goes when one is lost. Even at the height of spring a foggy night like this is dark.

My shoes filled up and I took them off lest they got left behind in the mud. I never became quite clear whether this horrible swamp covered a huge expanse of land or whether we kept on going round in circles in the morass. One thing was certain: we never got back to the Imperial again. Perhaps it had sunk. And then we suddenly stumbled across unmistakeable wheel-tracks that led out of this broad morass at one spot but seemed to have no connection with other roads.

Woman: This is the bog-dwellers' road to my home.

We now followed this path, endless at one end, in the direction that led away from the morass, and gradually reached drier going than there had been for a while, the ground between marshland and moor. Then sandy dunes with tangle and algae. Now it felt underfoot as if there were a slope a short distance ahead. I had my shoes under my arm and wiped the mud off them on the grass. I hadn't a dry stitch left.

All of sudden there was the turf of a homefield underfoot, and meadow-flowers growing in old farm-lanes. On a low grassy bank a farmhouse loomed through the fog.

We stood opposite the ribbed front of a little house with a turf roof. Sheep bleated at us from the roof. The living room window had six panes, but the window upstairs under the gable-head had four. The walls of the house were of turves that were long since overgrown. Once upon a time the gable had probably been red, then tarred, then limed; now much worn by wind and weather. In front of the window hung a faded piece of cotton that had received the sunshine of many a feeble summer.

This is my home, said the woman. I'm just going to pop in and wake mother and father and ask whether I can have a young man to stay the night with me. I'll make up a bed and tidy up the living room. I'm going to light a fire. Then I shall bake you some bread. Do please have a seat on the wall of the vegetable garden while you wait, my dear.

The house was unlocked and she opened the door and went straight in with her case and closed the door behind her.

The vegetable garden had not been dug yet and the dog had probably been hanged, because alien sheep were besieging the house. Under the farmhouse wall there stood a thicket of willow, birch, and angelica all intertwined, growing above the high withered grass; the old people had not had the energy to restore the fence, so the sheep cropped the leaves as soon as they sprouted. A ewe looked at me severely from under the thicket and bleated accusingly.

When I had hung about for a while out in the night rain I started wondering what the woman had meant when she whispered that we were going to the end of the world. Was it this place?

My fingers were so stiff I could hardly get my shoes on. What had become of the woman? Was she having so much difficulty in waking the old couple? Or was it so hard to get their consent for a young man to stay the night with her? There was no smoke coming from the chimney, either. Warm bread still seemed a long way off. Soon I had started shivering. Was I to perish of cold here, or what was I to do? Perhaps the best solution to the problem would have been to open the door, walk in, and go straight into the bed of the warm woman. Unfortunately no brilliant ideas occurred to me. I could not keep quiet and shouted in the direction of the house:

Where are you?

No reply.

I shivered and shook for a little while longer until I sighed hopelessly into the fog: Where am I?

But no reply. No sign of life at the house. At last my patience failed and I shouted out with all my strength of body and soul this one word, so that the alien sheep that surrounded the house shied away in terror:

Úa!

The reply to this extraordinary shout was a chilly cry from out of the fog like that of a great black-backed gull, and yet not that. When I listened more closely it sounded like laughter, and I recognised it: it was the woman in the other house. She laughed and laughed. The house laughed.

Your emissary crept away with his duffel bag in the middle of the laughter, but too stiff in the fingers to fasten his shoes. I was a little frightened. When I was out of sight of the house I took to my heels with my laces flapping about my ankles, and I ran as hard as I could back the way I had come. I was hoping that I would find the main road again.